Ploughing Songs

Damian Croft's stories have won numerous prizes and awards and have appeared in wide-ranging publications alongside such writers as Louis de Bernières. *A1 Northbound* won the Bill Naughton competition in 2000 and was subsequently published in *Splinters*. This is his first published collection. For the time being he lives in Italy.

GW00502873

DAMIAN CROFT

Ploughing
Songs

ELM TREE PRESS

Published by Elm Tree Press 2006

First published in Great Britain in 2006
by Elm Tree Press

A CIP catalogue record for this book is available from
the British Library

ISBN 0-9549827-0-3

Printed and bound in the UK by Biddles Ltd.

In Memoriam

Stephen Morley,

thatcher,

1946 - 2004

CONTENTS

Acknowledgement

Leaving school at eighteen, and with little idea of what to do with myself beyond some vague notions of poetry, I took a job with a local thatcher.

For the first week I was left alone in an osier bed near Godmanchester charged with the task of cutting thatching spars. The bed had once been coppiced for the withies used for basket-work in a local blind-person's home, but with the home now gone, some aggregate firm was digging it up for the gravel beneath. Each day, I worked ahead of the diggers cutting what osiers remained until, at midday, I wandered through the jungle of willow to the banks of the Ouse and swam across the river to a pub. I don't think I earned my pay that week and was subsequently demoted to tea-boy.

It was the beginning of a bizarre and unlikely summer, but together with Stephen Morley, I criss-crossed Huntingdonshire, encountering some of the most eccentric people I have ever met. Little thatching got done but a large friendship was cemented between us. These tales are pure adulterated fiction, but they hark from those days. They are inspired by episodes that happened to us, vague recollections of people we met, characters we heard about in pubs, a face glimpsed across a bar, an anecdote, a name.

I have Stephen Morley, thatcher, to thank for these stories, and for teaching me the way a story should be told.

Ploughing
Songs

Shitter Neil

Perhaps in some ways, Neil Linnell was unlucky, but no one thought about that till later.

On that breezy September morning at the Oxmoor Primary, headmaster Cullen stood facing the new intake seated cross-legged like angels before him. He was drilling a hole with his stare through a Linnell-like boy, head like a wing-nut, fists like sledge-hammers, reminding him of two elder brothers. Thought to his Scottish self, 'if you're a Linnell, then you must've done somat' wrong. And if you ha'en't yet, you're no doubt going to. So I'll punish you anyway'. And after that first assembly he gave the budding errant a taste of his new metre ruler. "F'r being a Linnell, m'lad!"

Neil Linnell's two elder brothers had tarred the family name irredeemably, even by Oxmoor standards, and Cullen was on the look-out right from the start. He wasn't going to let a third wash over him. He had his ways for dealing with such kids.

But Shitter Neil was not a nice kid. Even at the age of six. Had a way with his fists that poets have with words. Could write sonnets with those cuffs. Verse to get himself out of any tight corner. He didn't have friends. Didn't need them, he said. Instead he had confederates, other kids on the Estate who he bullied with his jack-hammer arms. Always bullying you for money on the way to school. Threatening a fight round The Dump at home-time, if you didn't cough up. Poking into your pockets with his rhyme-fisted punches. And some of us had it rough because of him. Our mums gave us our dinner money on a Monday morning and by the time we'd got to school Shitter Neil was smoking it round The Dump. We had to say we'd forgotten it. Teachers told us to bring it Tuesday. Back at home we told our mums the truth, and our dads beat us up for not standing up to the bully. But Shitter Neil was someone you couldn't stand up to.

His dad, Jimmy Linnell, ('Swanny' they called him, for reasons I never found out) had been a steel worker over in Corby but had been laid off just after Neil's fourth birthday. They'd moved to the estate for a new start, but like all the rest of us, had fallen victim to the Oxmoor rot. If you went for a job and told the gaffer you were living on the Oxmoor Estate, you wouldn't stand a chance. That was how it was in those days. And Swanny Linnell had a gammy left arm. Lost it in an accident in the steelworks. Couldn't drive a truck, steer a fork-lift, wheel a trolley, operate a JCB. Couldn't read and write, hold a pen, file a dossier either. Couldn't even pull a pint without a hand's-width head. No good to anyone. There weren't any jobs on the Oxmoor for one-armed bandits. Claimed what benefit he could. Tried to keep a lid on his temper and a thumb on his boys. But before long, the broken panes of glass, where Jimmy Linnell had smashed his angry right fist through living-room windows, became a regular testament to his burning inner rage. (That same rage which later, his children would carry with them into their classrooms, to vent verbally at morning prayers, carve in the lids of their desks, or with snot-pellets flicked at the teacher.) Then, after a year of taping up broken window-panes, Swanny Linnell got himself involved in a racket, stripping stolen motors and supplying a used-parts store. Must have been in it pretty thick because he spent ten years banged up.

As much for relief from her boys as for money, Mrs. Linnell took a job. Washing glasses in the Territorial. A Scouser, she smoked more than the Ferrybridge power station and larded her words with an accent no one on the Oxmoor could understand. The kids were growing up without a dad. And their mum was always with her hands plunged in soapy water, fag between her lips. Didn't seem to notice what her boys got up to.

It was his two elder brothers then, Clive and Dave, who brought Neil up. Both had been to borstal and had come out worse than when they'd gone in. No wonder Shitter Neil turned out like he did. Clive, tattoos like the vault of Ely Cathedral, and nose like a broadsword. He was eight years older than Neil and lorded over the Estate as if he was Hereward the Wake. Muscle-bound, his long hair trailing mane-wise behind him, and his beard carving the air like a cow-catcher as thunder rumbled from the cylinders of the Triumph Bonneville, which he steered like a long-ship through the ice-cold swells of darkest Huntingdonshire. Strapped to the back-rest of his bike was a long-handled axe, hickory-helved, blade glinting in the cold November sun. He was proud of that axe. Every few weeks 'Linnell's Chapter' descended on The Oxmoor like raiding

4

Danes. Hundreds of motorbikes, low-slung and shaggy, purred through the Estate like Shetland ponies. Handlebars like the horns of Highland cattle. Riders like Norsemen. And to herald their arrival, Clive Linnell, shoulders as broad as a farrier's, wielded his axe Viking-wise, outside the boarded-up door of an abandoned semi to plunder the vault of nine-inch brickwork, metal-frame windows, plasterboard ceilings. For a long-weekend, inspired by satanic ingestion of Fly Agaric, Hells Angels went berserk on The Oxmoor; evangelising, pillaging, raping, pissing, before bringing their rite to a suitably Nordic close and torching the ruin, fleeing drug-crazed into the fens. (Five years later Linnell the Elder was to get sent down for life after killing a Mod in a pub-fight Thrapston way. Made the poor soul drink his own blood from the jagged edges of a broken glass that Linnell thrust into his face.)

The middle brother Dave, face like a mug-shot, turned out even worse than Clive. Lacked his elder brother's flair for ritual destruction. Raked wanton maleficence wherever he went. Fought with flick-knives, knuckle-dusters, headbutts. Didn't share Clive's romanticism for symbolic tomahawks, just used raw cruelty. His fighting methods a repertory of unrefined brutality. Even Shitter Neil was scared of Dave, who beat him up frequently and unrepentantly, just for getting in his way. But he was the only kid I ever knew could ride a unicycle. Liked to show off with it. Appeared in the school review one year, the only time he ever came to school of his own free will. Ended up the star of the evening. Then he got big-headed. Rode his motorbike down the corridor outside the headteacher's study when he should have been in lessons. Expelled for good. By the time

5

his mum had got him into Hinchingbrooke he was past redemption. He'd already started on cars. Nicked from all over Huntingdon. But he pushed it all too far when he borrowed the headteacher's Cortina to practise hand-brake turns on the cricket square, before joy-riding it duck-wise into the Ouse at Houghton Mill. They sent him to borstal after that. (The last I heard of Dave he'd just been decommissioned from the tank regiment. Drove a Chieftain through the walls of the barracks).

In the Linnell family so it seemed, there was a kind of death-wish to upstage one's elders. But if Clive outshone Swanny and Dave outshone his elder brother, then Shitter Neil beat the lot of them.

As he got older, Shitter Neil got more and more obnoxious. Never smiled, just fixed you with his look. Had a stare like a socket-spanner. Growl like a Perkins-engine. Washed the Oxmoor slang round his mouth like gob, as if the words themselves were reasons to be bullied. Then spat his palatal-less utterances groundwards. Treading them in like dog-turd. Rode a Honda 125 which he kept running by siphoning fuel out of other people's tanks. Re-conditioned too, went like a greyhound on roller-skates.

No one dared ask him where he got that name of his and no one ever used it to his face, though he knew what we called him when his back was turned. (Only, you can be sure he never had the wit to figure out the way we stressed it. Shit 'n eel.)

Shitter Neil dropped out of school like a bird takes to the air. And no one ever chased him up. They were happy to let him truant. I guess the blot of unexplained absences on the school's records was a small sacrifice compared to the misery he caused the teachers and the rest of the pupils. By that time, despite even the Scottish headteacher's severity, Neil Linnell had outclassed even his brothers. When he finally gave up on school, he had more expulsions and suspensions to his name than most kids from Oxmoor went on to get CSEs. His grades? Four primaries, two secondaries, and one special school. All grade A expulsions. The last one for stringing a cheese-wire at neck height across the school-gate. Seven-thirty in the morning. Just as Roberts, the Deputy Head, was riding his bike into work. Was under intensive care for a week.

What he did with himself while the rest of us lived out their parents' dreams, only he knew. For a while he used to hang around the school-gate at four o'clock, bike parked across the alley, leaning over the handle-bars, mouth full of gum, like a bovine mascot. Got a spike haircut, wore a leather jacket with chains. Had that smell of all-day breakfast about him, like he camped out nights in the Greasy Spoon. Spat on the floor with the frequency of a dripping tap, the accuracy of a darts player, occasionally launching a slippery projectile sky-wards to fall ballistically, and arbitrarily on the head of any passing unfortunate. Had a gibe for anyone who passed within less than five yards, usually confined to a single syllable, two if he was feeling imaginative. Even the teachers on gate duty had to suffer his opinion.

n he must have figured out that dreaming up insults ry div that came out of the school gate was costing him too much effort. Took to tearing round the Estate on his bike, pulling wheelies for the panda cars, playing chicken with the oncoming traffic. Picked his victim from a hundred yards away. A law-abiding pensioner taking the wife on an afternoon drive, a Sergeant Major, car waxed with turtle wax, moustache with brilliantine, driving at a quick-march, or an L-plated teenager, clutching at the steering wheel for dear life, concerned parent beside them trying not to pedal the brake. Shitter Neil crossed over to the wrong side, hurtled full-throttle towards the approaching vehicle, head-down, open-mouthed, eyes screwed up like a lunatic, elbows sticking out like shark-fins. Said he liked the look of horror on the driver's face. Gave him a kick watching them panic, cover their eyes with their hands, crossing themselves, searching for the horn. Made out as if he was going to leap through their windscreen at sixty miles an hour. Right down their throats. Then swerved away within inches of his life. Timed to perfection, never once got it wrong. Then pulled on the front brake and swung round to tear up behind them again. Drawing level with the driver, waving his raging fist through the off-side window, swearing contempt as the old Sergeant-Major ragged on about him being a "Bloody Fool!". Then tore off into the sunset like a bad-dream.

Once he gave some poor sod a heart-attack. It was one Sunday morning over Papworth St. Agnes way. He roared up behind an old Ford Anglia navigating the country-lane like an oil-tanker in the Suez. Passed it on the near-side, fast enough to strip the paint from its wings, pushed on for quarter of a mile, then doubled back towards it. Only a narrow road, room for one car at the most. Hurtled towards the listing vehicle at the speed of a thunderbolt. Pushed the needle up to seventy then took his hands off the handle-bars. Spread them out as if he was a jet fighter taxiing for take-off. Then put his feet up on the handle-bars. Steering with his Dockers, arms outstretched, grazing the sky. They reckon the old sea captain was dead from a cardiac before Shitter Neil cruised past at seventy. He was back on the Oxmoor by the time the emergency services arrived to cut the cadaver from the wreck. Only witness was a man out walking his dog. Couldn't do a damn thing about it, he told the police later, utter lunatic he was! Shitter Neil never got caught for it. Should've gone inside.

Then he started sniffing glue. We used to see him with his cronies huddled up behind the garages where twenty years of Oxmoor history was graffitied on the brickwork. Plastic bags to their noses, warming the glue with their quick-working fingers. Breathing like dolphins. When questioned by detectives, the fish-brained iron-monger said he thought Shitter Neil must have found something useful to do. Never stopped to think why all of a sudden young Linnell was doing D.I.Y. that required so much regular investment in tins of adhesive. Never realised you could inject it, he told the cops. The rest of us knew better. Shitter Neil was the only one who kept 'Plus the VAT', as we knew him, in business. ('Plus the Vat' was a stumpy little man from Southend, kept little in his head, and even less on his shelves. Did a good line in bolt-croppers, replacement padlocks, heavy-duty chains, but not much else.)

It wasn't much afterwards when Shitter Neil got a tattoo. Rolled up his sleeve to show us. A snake it was. Someone said, "'n Eel more like," and we all ran away.

Then somehow, I never worked out why, Shitter Neil wanted to be my friend.

It started like this. I'd got into bunking off school whenever we had history. Hornet, the history teacher, somehow had it in for me and ever since the first year he'd heaped all his derision on yours truly. It was as if all the decades of his teaching had been in preparation for an attack on my ignorance. "Who was the famous diarist who once lived not five miles from where your behind is now parked?" he would ask in that sneering, Kings' College accent of his. Then, as if trying to drive a wedge into my skull, when I told him I didn't know, he would bring his text book sharply down on my head, once for each of the syllables, "Sam-u-el-Pepys you ig-nor-a-MUS!" Which was then followed by his oft-repeated only joke. "Boy! you're a feather of lead, what are you?" And I was supposed to reply, "an Oxy-moron sir." Then he rubbed it in even further with his sarcastic quip, "Another Ox-bridge candidate, in evidence, I see." But by the third year I'd got fed up with it and bunked off school every time we had history. But the police were always crawling around on the Estate and took you back to classes if they caught you, so I took to going fishing in the gravel pits beyond Brampton, up by the side of the A1.

I only had a Vespa and was still only thirteen. Not yet old enough for a licence and only supposed to use it off road, round the osier beds at Godmanchester, my dad said. But it was beyond my ken how I was supposed to get there without going on the roads in the first place. Then I worked out that beneath a helmet no one knew how old you were anyway so I just rode it on the roads as I pleased. The police never bothered with scooters as long as you didn't do anything stupid.

I was heading down the Arbury Road one morning, creel balanced on the pillion, rod pointing skywards, heady with the thought that Hornet wouldn't be cracking any of his Oxmoor jokes that day when Shitter Neil came screeching past me. Cut me up and made me pull over by the pavement. Gave me that kind of washed-out look he had in the mornings. Smelt of Greasy Spoon. Asked me where I was going. "Fishing," I told him plainly, hoping he wouldn't get any funny ideas about joining me. He laughed that toothy sort of laugh of his. Said he'd always fancied hunting sharks. Thought he might just tag along. Didn't have the guts to tell him no.

Said he'd race me there, but with my clapped-out Vespa, there wasn't even any point in trying, so I let him tear on ahead. It crossed my mind to change my plan and go to school after all, but even Shitter Neil's company was preferable to Hornet's. I'd always kept clear of Linnell since the day he rugged me at infant school, but after that, perhaps because of my elder brother Craig, he'd never given me much trouble. All the same, I considered it pretty strange he wanted to come fishing. Thought to myself there wasn't much chance of getting any bites with him around. Imagined he'd just start slinging stones in the water or pulling branches off trees. Or shooting up with speed. I passed by the school, keeping my eyes straight ahead. Didn't want anyone else to see me.

Heading out of Brampton on the Grafham road, there was little chance of meeting any traffic. Half a mile from Brampton the lane disappeared beneath a dense shade of willow trees and it was there that the gravel pits, obscured by the foliage, lived out their little-known existence. The road emerged into the open again only at the notorious intersection with the A1. Now there's a flyover, but in those days, the Brampton-Grafham lane bisected the Great North Road only with a tarmacked break in the central reservation the width of a barn door. For any motorist pulled up by the side of the A1 and waiting to cross, that car-sized lot was a heart-stopping leap away, glimpsed through a wall of two non-stop lanes of seventy-mile-an-hour lorries, trucks and London-bound motors. It was only a stepping stone before another mad dash between the bumpers of twin-laned and hell-bent vehicles got you on to the Grafham track. Nearly every other week, there was an accident there and the hazards of the crossing meant that the junction was as good as a dead-end. Most locals took a more life-preserving detour. The gravel-pits then, were almost always deserted, no one came by that way. The perfect place for a truant. They had been dug out in the sixties when the Great North Road had been upgraded from two lanes to four. Now, flooded and overgrown with willow trees and osiers, they were the long-forgotten and rarely fished property of the Hunts Fishing Club. (Which meant they never checked for permits and you could fish there all year without worrying.)

When I reached the gravel pits that morning, Shitter Neil's bike was already parked between the willows, concealed from view by the undergrowth. I thought I'd hear him a mile-off slinging debris into the water to scare off the fish. Instead, I came across him crouched down in the long grass on the bank, cigarette in hand, eyes fixed beneath the surface of the water.

"Blimey, there's baby dragons in 'ere, mate!" He beckoned me over and pointed out the pocket-sized amphibians swimming about. I put down my creel and rod and scooped one out with my landing net. Held the Great Crested Newt in the palm of my hand to show him it didn't breathe fire, showed him the flaming orange belly, the gecko-like jaw, then slipped it back into the water. Shitter Neil's eyes rolled over in disbelief. Had that kind of amazed, monkey-eyed look of childish incredulity. I set up my rod and tackle while he carried on staring into the depths.

"Nice roun' 'ere, innit?" words as sweet as honeysuckle from the mouth of Shitter Neil.

I pulled the lid off the maggot-pot. He grinned impishly. Must have liked the sight of them. I speared one onto the hook and cast the line into the water while Linnell pulled out a packet of Marlboros from the filthy lining of his leather jacket. All the years of acquired rage seemed to have been left behind on the Estate as he sat there in silence, staring at the float, the pond-skaters, the dragonflies, not uttering a word. Perhaps half an hour, three-quarters passed like that. I guess he was just happy to sit there in the company of someone to whom he didn't have to prove that his fists could talk. The float bobbed. I got a bite. Reeled in a carp. A real three pound beauty that rose out of the water like a genie. Shitter Neil started hopping about on the bank with excitement. Told me it was the most amazing thing he'd ever seen.

Later that same evening, back on the Oxmoor, he couldn't stop talking of that "fuckin' beautiful carp". Everyone thought he must have gone mad. Or taken too much speed.

Before the week was up, he was round at my house bugging me to take him fishing again. He'd got himself a rod and all the tackle. Nicked it from a guy in Godmanchester, ("fuckin' div-head"). I think my Dad got scared. He'd never objected to me going fishing, not even when he knew I should have been in school, but when he saw Shitter Neil turn up, he thought I'd started on the hard stuff and this fishing business was just an alibi for taking drugs or something. It took more than promises to talk him out of it.

After that, Shitter Neil came fishing with me almost every week, and in my own way I didn't mind him being there, he was company of sorts and kept you in beer, cigarettes and stories. But I still never quite worked out why he took to fishing like he did. Even knowing him later, the way he'd come up to you with a half-pound perch cupped in the basket of his hands, as if he'd just given birth to it, or the way he held a tench, gingerly between his fingers, a fishy look of wonder on his face, I never quite believed why such a tranquil activity attracted Shitter Neil like it did. He never killed a fish either. Said they were kind of sacred, and I remember once or twice, he even called me over to help him disgorge a hook. Couldn't bear to hurt a fish, he said. It was as if all his years of vicious rage and hatred for humans had manifested itself as a perverse affection for subaquatic life.

This other side of Shitter Neil though, was merely an eclipse. As soon as he'd packed away his rod and line, like the flip of a coin, he changed from the pensive Buddha to some madcap lunatic on a motorbike. Back on the Estate, he still bullied the other kids into giving him money, nicked all kinds of stuff from God-knows-where and terrorised the old ladies by riding past them on his motorbike and knocking off their bonnets. He still sniffed glue, shot himself up with speed, drank Tennents, carried a flick-knife. He was still the same old Shitter Neil, eyes always blood-shot, smelling of the Greasy Spoon, hair like a stickleback, the back of his neck studded with zits and tattoos growing up his arms like bindweed. His mad crazy self. Everyone thought I was nuts going fishing with Linnell.

Then it all came to an end. I remember it happened like this.

It was one of those long summer evenings, when the sun never sets. Shitter Neil and I had been sitting on the bank for what seemed like hours and nothing was biting. Both of us were bored. It was my idea.

"First one to swim to the island," I suggested.

"Oh, fuck off!"

I began to take off my shirt. "Last one there's a div!" (It was only later I found out that Shitter Neil couldn't swim.)

"Fuck it, let's play chicken!" Shitter Neil protested. "'Cross the A1 on the bikes."

I looked at him blankly.

"Three hundred yards run-up, straight across. First one to brake's a chicken!"

I'd heard of mad ideas, but never one as mad as that. True enough, at that time of evening the A1 was not especially busy, but there was no chance of getting across all four lanes of traffic.

"You must be joking! Do it yourself." I noticed his steel-green eyes cloud over with that vengeful distaste and I knew he was serious.

"Chicken! Only cause you daren't!" He began to roll up his sleeves. I knew he was aiming for a tumble. Perhaps if I'd have known then that he couldn't swim, I'd have headed for the island on my own. "You know what happens to chick, chick, chick, chick, chickens!"

He ran over to the road where his bike was and gave it a kick-start. He was heading straight for me. "Chick, chick, chick, chick, chickennnn!" He put his boot to my creel and sent it spinning into the water. I went livid with rage. By the time I'd pulled it out, soaked-through and tackle-less, he'd spun round on the bike and was coming back for me. He was too good a rider to hope he'd end up in the pit if I dodged him and he wore that look of insanity on his face. This time, as he roared past he whipped up my stool and rode off with it like a battle-honour. He braked and the back wheel skidded round so he was facing me again. I charged towards him; by now, tears were in my eyes. He flung my stool as far as he could into the middle of the lake.

"You bastard!" I screamed.

Shitter Neil span round, wheelied up onto the road and sped off towards Brampton. I ran to my Vespa. By now I'd forgotten what the taunt was all about and was intent on getting my revenge. I set off in pursuit. I was going to let him have it.

Three hundred yards up the road Shitter Neil braked and span round to face me. I spluttered up to him on my Vespa.

"You're a fucking nutter!" I roared at him, tears in my eyes, a lump in my throat.

He just grinned back.

"Wha' you gonna do about it, chicken?" he taunted. "Your turn first. You're the littl'un."

I hated him. I knew my Dad had been right to tell me to keep away from that monster. But there was no way now

I was going to back down. I was going to show him I wasn't scared, even if I finished up in hospital.

I span round to face the direction I'd come from. Two hundred yards ahead of me, the lane plunged into that shadowy throat of willow trees. At the far opening, where it emerged again to cross the highway, the setting sun balanced on the horizon framed between the goal-posts of the trees. Occasional cars passed in front of the glowing red ball. I watched a truck speed across, the gap winking for an instant like a tired eye. I counted to seven. A car went past. The gap in the trees winked again.

It was unfair from the start. My Vespa would only do forty at a push, his Honda would do seventy no problem. I revved up the bike and let out the clutch. I aimed at the sun, shining like a bulls-eye and when I roared into the tunnel of willow trees I was going at my all-out maximum. The needle showing thirty-nine. I hugged my elbows closer to my body and hunched my chin down to the level of the handlebars to reduce the drag. The needle inched its way to forty-three, then wouldn't budge further. Like a passenger, strapped into the crash-destined aeroplane already taxiing for take-off, there was nothing I could do. The crossing spread out in front of me, a runway leading to the sun-drenched sky beyond where the strata of cirrus were climbing step-wise. A car sped past, London-bound. Then another and a lorry heading North. I kept the throttle full on, the sun in my sights. Twenty yards from the Stop! sign a car flashed past. I still didn't flinch. Racing to catch up with the departing sun. I was so mad with rage that nothing would have stopped me. I shut my eyes and started to count to five. That was how long I reckoned it would take to get across.

The next thing I knew, I was hurtling through the air, flying arse over tit. I landed on my back and opened my eyes to find myself lying in the ditch, my Vespa, lying like a fallen horse a few yards away, its engine still running. I looked around and recognised the gravel pits on the far side of the highway. I leapt up and laughed. Not a bruise on my body. I waved to Shitter Neil, a quarter of a mile away back, already stepping on the gas.

From the Grafham side of the Great North Road you get a better view of the approaching traffic. Looking down towards Buckden, on the overpass two-hundred yards away I could see three lorries, one behind the other, pulling over the brow of the hill on the North-bound carriageway. I knew then that Shitter Neil was in trouble. A car passed on the South-bound carriageway. Then another. After that it looked clear, but the trucks on the Northbound were only fifty yards off the crossing. I could see he wasn't going to make it. But he'd made me go first and I wasn't going to rush out and tell him to stop. He'd do me over for making him the chicken. For a second I took my eye off the crazed motorcyclist, I tried to focus on the first of the truck drivers and by the time I switched my eyes back to Shitter Neil he was thirty yards off the crossing, his face screwed up into that gesture of mad defiance which he conjured up whenever he was going to do something out of his mind.

When the first truck drew level and obscured him from sight, I knew then he was dead. That vision of his mad-defiant face is the last picture I have of him. He hurtled out of the lane from between the trees into the South-bound carriageway and it must have been then that he caught sight of his suicide for the first instant. I heard the back wheel skid round as he pulled on the brakes.

The witness in the car heading south-bound said later, he'd seen some utter lunatic launch himself across the A1, then suddenly lose all control. Said he went skidding across the central reservation on his arse, trapped beneath the bike, right beneath the back wheels of the trailer of the Seddon Atkinson.

I heard only the screams of death, the thunder of an empty trailer, the squeal of air brakes and the almighty deafening sound as the third lorry swerved off the road and slammed into the ash tree by the side of the road.

But by that time I was on my way again. Wasn't going to let the cops catch me on my scooter.

A 1 Northbound

'Sausage, egg 'n' chips' was not the only reason why the Yaxley lay-by on the A1 Northbound was a mire of mud and a quarter-mile hedge of container-lorries. With curves like a cooling tower and tits like the Pennines, Vincenza Manciocchi came as a welcome break from the miles spent staring at some grubby tail-board used as palimpsest by anonymous wit. Her wild autumn hair caged behind her head and eyes dark as petrol, Vincenza had looks would not disgrace a goddess. And besides the best all-day breakfast on the Great North Road, she and daughter Mandi served a charm that was lacking from the canteens of the Little Thief and Happy Cheater. She had a way too with scrambling eggs and flipping omelettes that made truck-drivers go all gooey. Asked "do you wanta chilli-sauce?" as if she were singing Puccini. And the truck-driving classes were happy to confuse Puccini for sexual innuendo.

Athens-Redcar, Dusseldorf-Pontefract, Murcia-Doncaster all took the A1 Northbound. National road-freight bound for Edinburgh, Tyneside, Sunderland and York, local trucks carrying aggregate to Newark or collecting bricks from the factories at Peterborough all pulled off the Great North Road, just South of Norman Cross.

It was the sixties' scheme of straightening out the bends in the Great North Road, ploughing four straight lanes through open farmland, that left these tarmacadamed ox-bows in the roan Nene valley. For the most part, they were discarded as wasteland to be camped on by gypsies or used as dumping ground for hardcore by local builders. But the Yaxley lay-by was different.

The lower half obscured among the grass, the sign in the roadside verge already advertised promise:

Vincenza's Hot & Tasty
Snacks - 100 yards

Of a winter's day, a blizzard of truck-drivers huddled round a single charcoal brazier, scooping gobfuls of bacon rashers, runny eggs and mushrooms from plastic plates, already dreaming of seconds. Scoffed themselves with slices of fried bread and black-pudding, sausage and fried tomatoes, omelette-in-a-bun, chips and beans, cups of tea and coffee. Their talk of police-checks, strong winds, icy-roads and roadworks firmly arrested while they shamelessly stared at the two A1 beauties.

Vincenza's caff was nothing more than a caravan shaped like a Hovis loaf, long since retired from touring and now chocked up on breeze-blocks in the middle of the lay-by. The servery was a missing pane of glass and two orange propane cylinders standing adjacent to its flank doubled as urinal and ashtray. In the summer, a clutter of plastic garden furniture gave the truckers somewhere to sit, but in the winter they had to be content with standing.

But despite its appearance it had entered the road atlases of Britain's freight drivers as a listed building and undeterred by rain or snow, big men drew up at the lay-by in Seddon Atkinsons, DAFs, and Volvos, set their tachographs to 'rest' and stepped down from air-sprung seats and heated cabs, to stand in the freezing cold at Vini's hatch.

Queuing at the servery, they had as long as it took Vincenza to conjure up the sausage, egg and fried tomatoes to admire the geometry of daughter Mandi's neckline, the geography of her marvellous anatomy. Believed the money they invested in a mixed-grill platter a small price to pay for such a treat. But Vincenza kept her daughter Mandi strictly off the menu, knew all too well her darling progeny already flaunted the most appetising figure, bacon-hungry truck-drivers were likely to set eyes on.

Just seventeen, the product of an unprotected high-school love-tryst, daughter Mandi sent sixteen-stone men to the refuge of their cabs where they quaked in their dreams of imaginary conquests, guzzling down the milky tea from styrofoam beakers and scoffing bacon-sarnies. Then rubbed the shim of a coin with their fingers, deliberated going back for more, and wondering when the gaffer would next send them A1 Northbound.

Vincenza's mystique was her past. She had once been hooked up with a man who worked in the Peterborough

24

brick-yards, but clues to his identity finished there. How long she'd been in England, or why she came, no one ever knew. There were only guesses. And rumours.

But I suspect there were scarce few, staring at her beauty through the hatch of the caravan, would have guessed at the mundanity of her private life.

At five o'clock, her caravan shutters came down like dusk and she clasped shut the padlock that kept her restaurant closed till dawn. Then, at the wheel of an imagined Ferrari she drove her red Fiat Panda through the minor roads back to Peterborough, cursing her misfortune at having to prostitute egg and chips to make a living.

Home was a single-bedroomed flat, rented from Mr. Shah and smelling of soap-powder and automatic machine-dryers on account of the open-all-hours laundrette below. It was not much bigger than their caravan and the living-room no more than a cramped attempt at comfort, but it was their own small retreat from the world. Whether they lacked the company or whether they were just tired of making small talk after a day's cooking, I don't know, but Vincenza and Mandi never left their flat in the evening. Instead, robed in cheap cotton dressing-gowns, they slouched on the living-room sofa munching on takeaway pizza from the local kebab shop, drank saccharine orange squash from plastic beakers and lost themselves to the world of soap operas. If they talked, it was of the flower-arrangements, Christmas decorations, or of matching the colour of the table-cloth. And on Sundays, if they did anything at all, I imagine it wasn't much more than rearranging their statuettes of the Madonna and Christ round the living room - their little shrines to a better world that existed somewhere near Siracusa, in a forsaken corner of Vincenza's island.

And at night they slept together in the same double-bed, arms curled around each other, protecting one another from the insurgent mafia of truck-drivers firing pistol shots through the windows of their dreams.

Then in 1995, the licence for the café was not renewed. The Ministry of Transport had pushed through plans for that length of the A1 to be widened and upgraded to motorway and with their plans and legislation the roadside cafés vanished. Vincenza and Mandi moved out from their flat above the laundrette and I lost touch with them. I imagined they must have gone back to Italy.

But four years later, in a deserted lay-by on the A14 road, I came across the same tired-looking caravan I recognised from the Yaxley lay-by. I pulled up and wandered over to the hatch, doubtful that the famous Sicilian still owned it. I was surprised.

Vincenza had aged by more than the four elapsed years, squinted at me through a pair of ill-chosen specs and asked what I cared to drink. She hadn't recognised me. Her once autumn hair was flecked with grey and her proud shoulders, famous breasts had sunk. Her face more lined, paler, betraying a sadness, scowled as she slapped down the coffee and tidied my fifty pence piece into the till. She shoved a beaker of lumpy sugar beneath my nose.

Cradling the cup of brackish coffee in my hands, I reminded her I'd once lived in the attic above her flat in Peterborough. Her apology was genuine as she recalled me from the depths of her memory. I asked about business. Things were not the same she explained, in better English now. Besides the fiercer competition from the hamburger multinationals, her own drive to work had been blunted. A nasty affair with a Black Country crook had bruised more than her savings and confidence while a long court battle had improved her English but reduced her to financial zero.

"And Mandi?" I ventured.

She too had wounded her mother's heart. The victim of her own beauty, she'd worked as a dancer at a night club in Wolverhampton until she met a young man Dole who mistook his name as a licence to deal in drugs. Dole got her into substance abuse and the last Vincenza heard, her once lovely daughter was sharing a squat with a villain who saw it as his God-given duty to get the Birmingham youth on the waiting-list of the detox.

She complained that she'd had enough of the misery this island brought her. Said she was going to make enough to buy a villa back in Siracusa and then say good-bye to England for good. There was little hope hanging on here.

I looked at the forlorn lay-by passed by the incessant traffic and remorseless noise. I noticed the litter bin, with its two or three styrofoam cups and single Kit-Kat wrapper and concealed my thoughts that the coffee tasted of PG Tips and that the beaker looked recycled but unwashed. I chucked the whole lot towards the bin, hoping she wouldn't notice, then wished her good-day and told her I'd stop again the next time I was passing.

I headed back to my van, guilty of the lie that had just passed my lips. And wishing that four years earlier, when she'd knocked on my door late one night, it hadn't only been a pint of milk she'd been wanting.

Ploughing Song

Here are some figures about the village as it was back then:

- ☐ thirty-five households
- ☐ an electoral roll of seventy-seven
- ☐ twelve children still at school.

And here are some facts about the things we didn't have:

- ☐ a vicar
- ☐ a village stores
- ☐ a school
- ☐ a pub
- ☐ street-lamps
- ☐ drains.

And as I remember finding out, there is no mention of the village in the pages of the Domesday Book - a matter I contend is an oversight, since parts of the church predate the survey. The pub was closed down in the fifties after word got round that the returning drovers used it to give a bad name to a few otherwise nameless women, and if one discounts the unmetalled drift-road once used by sheep drovers, there was only one through road (metalled 1965) - which traversed the old airfield en-route to Spaldwick.

This then, is an inventory of things as I remember them:

☐ one old church
☐ seven farms (including one pig farm)
☐ six thatched cottages
☐ eight semi-detached council houses
☐ a village room (the inside of which we never saw)
☐ a stone cross (fallen down) on the village green
☐ a well (blocked up), also on the village green
☐ seventeen or so mature field elms
☐ three decent conker trees
☐ eight or nine good ponds.

And here (also from memory) is a list of the delivery vans that in those days regularly passed through the village:

☐ the postman
☐ the milkman
☐ Hall's bakery van
☐ Brown's the chemist
☐ Twigden's mobile grocery store
☐ Appleby the butcher
☐ the dry-cleaner's
☐ the Huntingdonshire mobile library service
☐ the coal-lorry (in winter)
☐ the ice-cream man (in summer)
☐ the fish and chip van.

Whilst more occasional services were:

- ☐ the farrier
- ☐ the knife-grinder (who also dealt with lawn-mowers)
- ☐ gypsies hawking clothes pegs
- ☐ the sludge-gulper.

Little else, beyond the slow unfolding of the seasons, ever seemed to happen in the village. Life was elsewhere. I myself left at the first opportunity and after my parents moved to St. Neots I had little reason to return.

It was only on a whim then, that I last week paid a visit to the place where I was born and only by chance therefore that, strolling down the lane past the churchyard and noticing the fresh turf laid over a new grave, the name on the hasty wooden cross, I was reminded something did happen. Once.

Shy as money in a miser's pocket, George Stokes kept himself to himself, hardly ever said a word to anyone, and no one, out of deference to his habit, ever asked. They knew the isolate syllable he lavished on the world from time to time had cost him precious effort and didn't press him further. Only Graham Barlow, his neighbour, had ever heard him turn a full sentence. Said he had a voice like a diesel engine, a slow, regular purr that called to mind a John Deere tractor.

Stokes lived alone for as long as most folk knew him, though there were several remembered his mother, and a few recalled his father Wally, who'd tumbled drunkenly from a hay rick when his son was three years old.

He had left school at fourteen and gone straight to work on the farm. His mother needed the money, and he didn't need the inconvenience, he'd told the headmaster, by way of explanation. Besides, he could already drive a tractor better than the Maths master could keep discipline, and the Chemistry master could do successful experiments. He knew how to write his name, count the seasons and keep silent. That was all he needed to make his way in the world. And working for Vaughan on the farm, he took home a small wage that afforded him and his mother a hot bath once a week and to burn coal as well as wood on the fire in winter. Then his mother died of a heart-attack and Stokes was left an orphan at twenty-one. He took a housekeeper, Mrs. Gable, who went once a week to do the cleaning, washing and to cook a simple hot-pot, but Stokes drew the line at her moving things around. Home, after Mrs. Stokes' death, was a place to keep the memories of his mother.

Stokes barricaded loneliness, quietitude, emotion from his soul by way of a singular, life-consuming hobby. I doubt it was a solution he'd meditated on, just one he'd arrived at with the slow, inevitable passing of years. As if it were a smouldering vocation that welled inside him like unquelled violence.

Returning from a day of ploughing, he would shut himself away in his shed, and amidst the failing lamplight, warmed only by an ancient paraffin heater, sit hunched over lathe or rasp to dedicate himself to valves, cylinders, piston-rods, parts small as cogs in a wrist-watch. To those who knew of his devotion, it seemed strange that such a large, bear-like man, with his spatulate ploughman's fingers should chose to work in miniature, but it was a contradiction I imagine Stokes himself never would have contemplated.

There were few in any case who knew of Stokes' pastime, his patient dedication to building model steam engines. He showed his work to no one, had no instinct for trying to impress and shared his satisfaction with his own inner self. Most of us found out about it only later.

And I doubt very much if Stokes ever did anything else with his spare time. He didn't take a newspaper (as I found out when I did the paper round), his roof was one of few that didn't have a TV aerial and there was no phone-line either, to judge from the lank wire straggling from the telegraph pole outside his house. Instead, his life was fixed on a reverie dreamed around the effect of Boyle's laws, a lifelong meditation on a bucolic past and an existence dedicated to a bygone world of agricultural engines.

We saw Stokes only rarely. By the time we left for school in the morning, he was already at work, harrowing some field in the far marches of the parish and my only memory of him is of Saturday evenings, waiting in the queue for the fish and chip van.

Where the knot of mothers gathered of an afternoon awaiting children from the homebound school-bus, impatient feet had scoured a hollow in the roadside verge. This muddy patch served the village well enough as bus-stop and, except in the long summer holidays when it recovered a little green, epitomised the maintenance programme of the local council.

It was here that on Saturday evenings, the five or six men sent forth from their families stood like a clump of hazel stools, clutching the empty pyrex dishes to their chests, turning over stones with the toes of their shoes and waiting for the arrival of the fish and chip van. The roll-call was always the same. Doddy Waters - apprentice joiner, Graham Barlow - garage mechanic, Jack Dawe - window-cleaner, Isaac Hunt - odd-job man, George Stokes - farm-hand, my father - school-teacher, and myself, who my father took along to help carry home the chips.

Football never generated much passion among the hearts of the slow-willed villagers. If it was winter, they talked of ploughing or chain-saws. If it was summer, the nuisance of wild oats in the seed mix, the hope of a clear spell, the chances of a good harvest. One year though, it was all Dutch Elm. And another year, fingers curled round the two or three suspect one pound notes, the recent invasion of decimal currency in their pockets. (As Isaac Hunt would pontificate, "can't see the point in decimals, or what's so vulgar in fractions.").

Only George Stokes never spoke, stood apart from the rest and clutched in his arms a round enamel wash-basin - receptacle for a week's suppers of reheated double cod and chips.

It was always ten to six when Ella's sea-green van came into view, sounding its signature tune as it drew through the cutting, crawling up the shallow incline like a Trojan Horse and with smoke and chip fat pouring from the chimney. Ella's great smile beamed through the windscreen and the van would pull to a halt by the clump of men before she heaved her weight from the driving seat to push her way through a small doorway into the kitchen compartment behind. Sliding open the sash window she expelled into the dusk great wafts of chip smell and hot, steamy air.

"Evnin' gents."

"You alright?"

"Not so bad, an' you?"

Ella was a big girl. Not old at forty-one, but years of over-eating had made her bloom to the shape of a King Edward potato and now the folds of her neck were threatening to submerge her chin.

Oil unchanged for several years at a time, she lorded over those two vats of hot fat in the back of her van, like they were disobedient school-children, fished the battered cod from their depths like they were hands held out to be slapped. Then trawled a wire sieve for the limp and greasy chips sunk to the bottom like detritus, tossed them in the drying rack, let them drip the pints of precious oil back into the fat-vat. No one ever told her she was driving a bomb. What with the oil-vats leaking fat within an inch of the flame of the gas burner beneath. But then, those were before the days of the Common Market's intervention in affairs of caution.

Stokes was always first to be served, I don't know why. He held out his wash-basin for Ella to fill with the five pounds of chips and half dozen battered cods and had-docks that would constitute his suppers for the next three days. It was always, "two thirty-five the lot, love" and he sprinkled his change on the Formica-topped counter before her, let her count the filthy coins with the same hand that sliced the potatoes and battered the cod. No one ever complained.

Stokes never got the hints Ella dropped him; the extra portion of chips, the slice of cod, a pickled egg or an extra-large smile. And it never crossed anyone else's mind either that the fish and chip lady was pining after Stokes like he did after her chips. Or, that at night-times Ella's unagile mind dreamt of Stokes…

…until that February night in '75.

It was a Sunday morning when the tryst was discovered. Jack Dawe, out with his dog to watch the snow drifting off the airfield, saw Ella's fish and chip van parked up by the railway cottage. He thought, at first, she'd had to leave her van in the village for fear of getting stuck in the drifts. The snow that previous evening had been heavy and the road across the airfield had been closed, but the road through the cutting, in the other direction was still passable. Then, later, Dawe noticed the curtains in Stokes' terraced cottage still drawn shut and recalled that Stokes, by habit, was an early riser.

Despite the thaw that came two days later, Ella's fish and chip van didn't move all week and Stokes sent word round to Vaughan he was struck down with 'flu. They were the first days of illness Stokes had ever taken and no one in the village believed him, whispered he was ploughing other furrows. And for a week, the village feasted more on the gossip of George Stokes and Ella Flack's proverbial agriculture than it ever had on Ella Flack's chips.

It came to an end though the following Saturday, when Steve Flack, Alconbury builder and Ella's husband, turned up to retrieve his errant wife. He'd been searching the county for a week before he heard about Ella's chip van parked in the village and suspected its inertia had less to do with snow drifts or mechanics, rather more to do with adultery. And Flack wasn't a man to have the mother of his two sons running off with a ploughman ten years her junior, knew he'd have to put a stop to it somehow. He put an axe through Stokes' front door and dragged his laughing, naked wife from the stairwell. Then bundled Ella into the back of his builder's van like she was a delivery of bricks and drove off at full pelt. He didn't give a damn about the fish and chip van. It wouldn't be doing any more rounds, that was all he knew.

Stokes' influenza took a long while getting better after that. He took another week off work. Then another. Then Mrs. Gable got told she didn't need to show up again. By the time a month had gone by, Vaughan on the farm was beginning to wonder when he'd see his ploughman again and had to send Graham Barlow round to talk Stokes out of his condition. It was then that the truth emerged.

Apparently, it was after dark when Ella'd knocked at Stokes' door. Said her chip van was stuck in a drift and asked point blank if she could stay the night. Stokes had tried to suggest he could fetch a tractor off the farm and tow her out, but Ella didn't want to hear of such a favour. He made her up a bed on the sofa but had the fright of his life an hour later when she appeared, naked and luminous at the door of his bedroom, intent on assaulting his privacy. Couldn't get a word in edgeways as she bounded into bed and began the week of lovemaking she hoped would be the start of their affair. On the Sunday morning, exhausted from the haddocking she'd given him, Stokes had overslept. It was midday when he finally made it downstairs to open the curtains, but knew by then, it was already too late. All the village would know that Ella Flack had battered more than just cod between the covers of his single bed.

Couldn't face the shame of what had happened. Thought it best to keep his curtains drawn.

By the next day, when Ella showed no signs of moving on, he was already a prisoner of his own shame. Knew he couldn't face the village litigation, but knew the longer he stayed shut up with Ella, the worse it would all be. Was relieved to hear the sound of Steve Flack's axe making splinters of his front door.

Stokes was condemned by the shame of what he'd done. In his gentle mind, he saw the villagers tear strips from him every time he walked out of his front door. He never understood it wasn't a crime to spend a night with a woman and had the strange idea he'd been dubbed a monster in the village just cause he'd seen Ella's jumpy body. And though he went back to work after Graham Barlow's counsel, I doubt if Stokes ever really got over what had happened. We never saw him after that. Except for going out to plough Vaughan's land, without occasion now to wait for fish and chips, Stokes never again left his shed of steam engines.

Seeing the fresh turf on the grave, I went to search out Barlow; certain he would know how Stokes died. By chance, I found him at the back of Stokes' cottage clearing out the shed.

"It were two weeks back. He'd ploughed the whole of Bunker's Crest that morning and was just turning back to plough the headland, alone but for the gulls that followed in his wake, when he fell from the tractor clutching at his chest. Whoever was going to hear the dying man's cries for help out there? He only got as far as the ditch. And it were the afternoon before a girl on horseback found him lying face down in the soil, a flock of peewits wheeling over-head."

Barlow led me round the corner to the yard where the opus of Stokes' life was laid out on the concrete screed.

"What a bloody shame," Barlow cursed. "And none of us ever knew about it."

Seventy, eighty, maybe a hundred scale-model steam engines crammed the small yard. Farm traction engines, steam ploughs, road rollers, steam pumps, piston engines, all painted in authentic colours.

There were tears in Barlow's eyes as he reached down, lit an oblong meths burner and slipped it beneath the boiler of a polished brass steam engine. He disengaged the clutch, let the boiler build up steam, then walked me round the rest of the collection. Showed me how the whole of Stokes' life had been dedicated to this silent hobby of making steam work. I stood back, wondered at the hours of loneliness Stokes had invested in its making.

I pictured Stokes alone in his shed, his eyes focused on the job before him, his thoughts closed to the outside world, his inner world one of flanges, trunnions, knuckle-pins and cotters, machining a fly-wheel till it turned like spring on the heels of winter.

"Had no family to mourn for him," Barlow sighed. "And the clump of villagers gathered round his grave - Jack Dawe, Isaac Hunt, Doddy Waters, myself - brought to mind how over twenty years ago we were all stood beside the road of a Saturday evening, awaiting Ella's chip van. Talking of ploughing. Or chainsaws."

The boiler had built up steam, Barlow released the throttle and gave the fly-wheel a gentle nudge. I watched the engine slowly acquire momentum, the piston muscling the piston rod forwards and back, elbowing the crank shaft into motion. Steam was spitting from the piston exhaust valve and the polished brass fly-wheel was turning on its axle. In a single, mesmerising motion.

But driving nothing.

Working, only for the sake of working.

Sitting here now, writing all this down, I can't drive that image from my mind: A fly-wheel, turning only for the sake of turning. A sorry, apposite metonym for the life's work of George Stokes - model-maker.

Slip Jig

At the Strawberry Fair on Midsummer Common, a group of truants from the school tennis tournament robed in kaftans and beads, passed round a joint and thought nothing of Monday's exams. They were heady for adventure and of the mind it would come quicker if they left their minds elsewhere. One of them, Jessica, a flower-spangled girl of nomad fantasies, fabulous ideals and exuberant hair, was bored with waiting for the improbable and thought she'd go in search of her destiny. Sixteen years old and a day-pupil at a reputable Cambridge public school, she threaded through the weft of drunken bodies with eyes alight for any single male with a jug full of beer who was happy to share it with a schoolgirl.

She angled through the stalls of artisans and craftsmen, stone-polishers, potters, wood-turners, and mosaicists, wandered past the stalls of poets who wrote verse to order and the astrologers who made horoscopes (also to order) and thought it highly unlikely she'd find adventure there. She kept on past the jewellers, hatters, vegan soap-sellers, T-shirt printers and the large-bosomed zingara inviting punters into her tent to walk the tips of her fingers across their hamburgery palms and encourage them to return to her later to seek out a different kind of fortune.

She was on the point of turning back when, beside the avenue of limes, she saw a gypsy caravan, its horseshoe arch of green tarpaulin sleepily anarchic to the rest of the festival. Beside it, a pony took Midsummer Common at face-value and was grazing contentedly while a dog slept off the heat in the shade. In front of it was sat a smokey, bearded hippy, hammering a punch into a leather belt, and every now and then, combing back the dreadlocks of his hair with his hand.

"This is nice," Jessica said as she felt one of the leather masks hanging amongst the display of belts, bags, purses, key-rings.

The hippy pulled up a stool and bade her sit down, asked if she was interested in leatherwork, spoke in slow arching sentences, with thick dusky syllables exposing the vestiges of a Lincolnshire accent.

Jethro was a man who lived outside The System. He had never paid tax, drawn the dole, held a licence, or opened an account. Neither had he ever consulted a doctor or had his teeth pulled. He'd burnt his National Insurance number the day he'd received it and since the age of eighteen had lived without an address. Reckoned he was as damn near anonymous as was possible in this fascist police state of modern Britain. Only wished to God his birth had never been registered, but had been too small at the time to do much about it. And whenever the police stopped him on the road he always used a false name, of no fixed address.

He nursed a paranoia of ever getting his name on the state's computers and kept away from city centres, shopping malls, garage forecourts, traffic lights. Anywhere, in fact, where he suspected there was closed circuit TV. Said that one day he would be paid back for his endeavours not to pay tax, collect the dole or payments for health. He had the fixed idea, that human kind was better off without the State.

"Like, where's the law says a person *has* to belong to a State? You know what I mean? Like, they can't *make* you be English, can they? Not if you don't want to be."

Palestinians, Kurds and gypsies. All of them lived without protection of a State. And to Jethro's mind they were better off for it. "It's the State that fucks you up, man. Ties you to a piece of land you feel desperate to defend. The cause of wars. You know what I mean? Like, in the twenty-first century, States, Countries, Nations are all gonna become a thing of the past. Like people are gonna recognise they don't have need for them. See... it's boundaries, man. Borders. People think borders just mark the end of one country, the beginning of another, like. But... it ain't. Like, imagine a map of the world, blank except for the borders. What's it look like? A net! Yeh, a net. To catch people. And that's just what borders are for. To stop people moving around, just 'cause they haven't got a passport. You get what I mean? But soon people are gonna find ways of gettin' over those borders. You know what I mean? Like, they won't stop me and Shanks hitting the road... and travelling wherever we want..."

Jethro's thesis was a crowded platform of blind Irish harpers, peasant English poets, Cherokee Indians,

Romanian tinkers, Hindu gods and Islamic freedom fighters, all of whom, according to Jethro, fought for the ascendance of a gypsy way of life. His argument was a tangled cosmography explaining a disparate humanity progressing towards a common destiny of the Romany way. It was a confused and intricate dream in which John Clare linked hands with the descendants of Cain to espouse a lifetime of running away.

"And that's why," Jethro went on, "when the world wakes up and sees the State's a thing of the past, all those people with pension funds, healthcare programmes, who live off the social, you name it… they're gonna lose everything. Everything, man."

Jessica stared at him with her dreamy eyes as if he was a miracle-worker and when dusk fell and the stall-holders began lighting their lamps, Jethro took a flagon of cider from his caravan and suggested they share it. He didn't drink much, he said, but her company was a good excuse to make the exception. He packed away his wares and invited her to join him in his caravan, showed her to a seat on a bunk draped with a thick Afghan rug. Then he turned down the Tilley-lamp till it drew just enough light from the shadows and placed it by the hob of the stove. Told her they were destined to life on the road together. And Jessica felt their lives knit together like a zip.

Long past midnight, she gathered her clothes from the caravan floor and guiltily remembered her parents, the now-broken promise to be home by eleven. Jethro took her in his arms and asked her to join him on the road. She explained pathetically she had school exams to finish first, but taking paper and pen from her pocket, she scribbled her address, said she'd be finished in a fortnight, he should write with his whereabouts. She'd come and find him.

"You know they check the mail? I don't usually go writing letters, like."

"Use a code name. Sign it with the name of your pony. I'll know who it's from."

Then she slipped away through the remains of the night and the litter of the fair, unaware of the terrible hole she had made in the gypsy's heart.

It was a Saturday morning two weeks later when Jessica left her house in Victoria Road with a duffel bag of old clothes, violin and tattered book of folk tunes, trying not to imagine her mother watching suspiciously from an upstairs window. She walked briskly towards the station, untroubled by the lie to her parents about a week's conservation work on the Norfolk Broads. She would write to them on Monday saying the Trust was short of volunteers and she'd elected to stay on for the summer, would see them all again in September.

It was raining when she got off the train at Holt and she still had another mile to walk to the field where Jethro had told her he had parked his caravan.

Jethro was sitting in his caravan, hunched over his leather-work, when he noticed the umbra shift in the outside light. Looking down, he saw a ragged sylph standing up to her knees in the wet grass. He laid aside his work and leapt down from his caravan to throw his arms around her. They climbed the steps to his caravan and crawled into the smokey darkness. The stove was burning and Jethro put a pot of water on to boil, prepared the mugs of wild sage tea. He didn't drink caffeine and the tannin in tea was bad for you, he explained. Not to speak of the exploitation of tea-pickers, all women, in Sri Lanka and India, he went on. Better to glean what one could from the hedgerows of rural England.

For three days Jethro laid aside his leatherwork while he and Jessica spread themselves out on his Afghan rug and hid themselves from the drizzle pattering on the tarpaulin roof above them. Occasionally he stirred to make a pot of sage tea or to poke the embers of the stove, and they paused to eat only when their love-making had sapped every last bit of strength from their limbs. Jessica snuggled her face into Jethro's hair and thought of her school friends, all getting summer jobs in accounting firms, on holiday with their families in the Dordogne, or going on tennis camps in Sussex. Knew they'd all be going back to school in September, to carry on their boring lives. Knew she'd done right in becoming a gypsy.

A cuckoo sounded its staccato cucks somewhere in the woodland beyond, the poppies swayed in the breeze and Jethro was once again hunched over his leather work.

Jessica sat down in the long grass to write to her parents. She told them she was happy and that she was working hard for the conservation volunteers. There was a lot of work to do and she was thinking of staying on for a while. She couldn't leave them an address as they were constantly moving from site to site depending on where they were needed. They shouldn't worry about her, she'd be back home in time for school in September. And her sun tan was coming on tons. It was a mildly non-committal letter, the kind she could easily back out of later.

Then, for the first time since she'd arrived, she took her violin out from its case, spread the book of tunes on her lap, leafed through to find a reel she knew, then brought the violin to her neck and began to fiddle. The Tarbolton came hoodling out of the violin, faster and faster. She played it over and over, until the notes began to fit together like the pieces of a jigsaw, the eight bar phrases locked like a ruler in her memory. In the bright afternoon air, fuelled by the excitement of a new love, she felt the violin light beneath her chin, the notes flowing out like water. And she remembered her violin teacher Dold, in love with Brahms and scales, and thought how he would have scoffed at the folk music. It made her play faster, wilder, more carelessly until the vibrato she had invested so much time in acquiring had all but vanished. She imagined Dold's voice in her ear. "What sort of noise is that, my girl?" and she laughed out loud. Realised she *could* play the violin after all.

That summer, they travelled from one festival to another. Jethro seemed to have a circuit of them mapped out in his head. And as soon as one of them finished, they hit the road again for the next. It was a way of structuring their existence, and it gave Jessica something to look forward to. In between, they travelled slowly, life took its time - Jethro leading his pony Shanks by the bit and whistling to his dog Tennyson, Jessica walking alongside the caravan, or riding on the footplate. Her hair was growing wild and great long strands of a clematis-like mane flowed round her punky pre-Raphaelite face.

At the festivals, they parked the caravan among the stall-holders, tethered Shanks where he could graze in peace and Jethro would set up a small stall outside his caravan to work at his leatherwork whilst the light was good.

Jessica hid herself inside and played the violin. Whereas at school she had practised for half hour a day at the most, now she played until her arms were so sore she could no longer hold the instrument to her chin. She was gaining in confidence, had lost that ugly vibrato that hid her wrong notes, and had acquired instead a careless glissando that gave her playing a wild, herby feel. Her playing had a lightness it had never had before, as if it were some effortless gossamer floating in and out of her mind, the notes lilting on the bed of her imagination instead of being herded towards some awkward and ill-fitting cadence.

In the evenings there were always camp-fires, joints passed round and drink to be had. If there was music, Jessica was always among the musicians, improvising a melody to whatever chords the acoustic guitars battered out. Otherwise she would resign her violin to its case for the evening and lose herself to the recklessness of drinking, passing joints among the dropouts, punks and hippies.

At the end of August Jessica wrote another letter home. It was as vaguely worded as the last and written with a pen she'd had to borrow. She told her parents that she no longer believed in the material world, she had found peace and inner happiness and as a result she would not be returning to school that September. But they shouldn't worry about her. She was getting on fine and playing the violin lots. They could even send her best wishes to old Dold (if they could rouse him from his coffin that was).

But with the passing of summer, the festival circuit came to an end, and with it, Jethro's meagre income. They did a bit of apple picking and there was talk of some decent work when potato picking started, but otherwise they were left on their uppers. It was true, they didn't need much money between them. Jethro got hold of whatever they needed to eat by scrumping from kitchen gardens and by fetching the odd rabbit from the hedgerow.

Jessica took to busking. Whenever they passed near Norwich, King's Lynn, Cambridge, Stowmarket, Jessica would foot it into the town centre to busk. She was becoming a powerful player of the jigs and reels and she could make people lilt in the street as they walked past, tipping pound coins into her upturned hat. She made good money busking. Sometimes sixty pounds in a day.

She longed to drag Jethro into Cambridge for an evening getting drunk on the money she earned from the hat, but Jethro would never go with her. His response was always the same.

"You're gonna pay for all this one day, man. Everytime you stand up in Red Lion Square, they've got closed circuit cameras trained on you. They see every pound coin that goes in your hat. They've got you fixed up, man. Know exactly how much money you've been earning. And one day they're gonna send you the tax bill. And it's gonna hurt."

"Oh, don't be stupid Jethro. Even if they do, so what? Why's it gonna stop you coming into town for a night?"

"And get myself bar-coded as I get on the bus to come home, right? You gotta be joking! I've kept myself anonymous this long. I'm not going to blow my cover now."

But during the winter things got hard for Jessica. With no festivals to travel to, and Jethro not keen on going into town, their social life dragged to a standstill. She was still happy with Jethro, and in his own gentle company they worked their way through the long winter nights, he at his leatherwork and she at the violin.

It was hard sitting it out, day by day in the caravan. And busking she had to wear mittens to stop her hands freezing up. From time to time, she got gigs in folk-clubs, not well paid but at least she got an evening's beer from the deal and a chance to sit in the warm and talk.

She and Jethro lived on the road together for another two years. But it was an autumn afternoon in Norwich that the bombshell exploded in Jessica's life. She was busking outside the cathedral. Beautiful slip jigs sliding from the bow of her violin. A small crowd was beginning to gather round her and were tossing pound coins into her hat like they were chewing gum wrappers for the bin. Faces came and went from the crowd, but there was one that didn't change. It leaned against a pillar on the far side of the streets and admired the music. When Jessica had exhausted her repertoire of folk-tunes she thanked the people standing round and bent down to collect up the money from her hat. It was then that the young man stepped forward from the opposite side of the street. He was a tall man in his thirties, balding, and wearing a smart tailored suit with a silk scarf wound round his neck. And he asked her if she fancied a beer.

As they strolled towards a pub, he flattered her with compliments on her playing. It was quite the finest folk fiddling he'd heard in years.

Later, in the pub, he introduced himself as a music producer. He had a band in London laying down some tracks for a new album and asked her how she would like to play on it. She'd be paid as a session musician and would be required for a week. The flat rate of pay would be a thousand pounds - but always of course with the possibility of more work afterwards. And with a face as pretty as hers, there was no reason why she shouldn't be considering a solo career in the future. It was the step that could launch her career. Folk music's just taking off, he explained.

That night, huddled in their caravan over a bowl of rabbit stew, Jessica told Jethro of the producer's offer.

"Why don't you come to London for the week? You could come in disguise, put Shanks in the stables, Tennyson in the kennels. I'll pay for everything."

"Fascist city bastards. Work for guys like that and you've sold your soul down the line. You become a part of The System. Another cog in the wheels of our fascist police state. You go and work for that guy Jessica, and yeh, you'll earn a grand but you'll lose your freedom. Freedom, man. What's more valuable to you? The money or your freedom?"

"But Jethro, it could be the start of my career."

Jethro couldn't swallow another mouthful of the rabbit stew. The lump in his throat had grown too large. And tears were already welling in his eyes.

"You never were a real gypsy, Jessica."

And, the next morning, as Jessica set foot on the London bound train, her duffel bag of old clothes slung over her shoulder, her tattered book of folk-tunes now all in her head, and her violin tucked under her arm, she knew deep down that her life on the road had finished. And that she'd broken a gypsy's heart.

Forty Foot Drain

It's a rainy kind of April day in '71, when a young Noah Lot, face like a three-quarter moon turns up in the pub in Littleport asking if anyone has a plot of land going spare. Beside him, Nora, a nervous, mackerel-shape of a girl, older by a decade and with a face hollowed out by years of substance-abuse, stands staring wildly at the locals. Her relationship to Noah is open to suggestion and the lack of words between them, makes it difficult to guess. Where they might've sprung from is another matter of conjecture, but when fenman Thomas Mobbs hears there's someone in the pub looking to buy a plot of land, he orders a round of double whiskies for the visitors. In his devious mind he's got the fifty acres of floodland abutting the Forty Foot Drain he's been wanting to be rid of for years. Passes two single-malts down the bar, says he knows just the piece of land they might be after. Couldn't find more fertile soil, if you spent another year looking. Speaks liberally of phosphates, nitrates, and countless other 'ates and is damned if he'll be parted with it, but he's got the taxman on his back for capital gains and he's got to raise the dosh to pay him somehow. He forks out a rare penny for the half-bottle of scotch with which he laces Lot's mind and bides his patient time till he sees the strangers totter on their stools, then suggests a drive out to the fen to have a look.

They tumble out into the late afternoon air, thick with starlings and mist, to climb into the fenman's ageing Land-Rover. With one hand on the wheel, the other searching the ashtray for a lengthy dog-end, Mobbs says it's only the rain they've been having lately has made his field a touch muddy. Conceals the fact the bogland is good for little else but boating and catching eels and in winter when it freezes, ice-skating.

Noah Lot doesn't know much. It was the previous summer when the apprentice panel-beater, nineteen years old and a life ahead of him, was hammering out a wing on an Austin Maxi when a hoist gave way and the engine suspended above him knocked the last bit of sense from his head. He got twelve thousand pounds from the garage owner and permanent damage to his cerebral cortex. Rendered him vulnerable to memory lapse and disorientation.

With an eerie lucidity however, he knows he's now a dimwit and hasn't a hope of ever holding down another job. Knows too the twelve thousand pounds he received in compensation has got to last a lifetime but knows nothing of investments, unit trusts and shares. Doesn't want to languish on the social for the rest of his miserable life. Or stay at home with Mum and Dad like a house-cat. Has to find a way to live somehow and his plan's a simple one: he's gonna buy a few acres and live off the land. Reckons he has just enough wits left to hoe a crop of turnips, keep a few goats and chickens, maybe a pig. Knows too what folks have told him: the Fens aren't as pretty as Wiltshire, Devon, Norfolk. But if you're short on marbles, and keep your eyes on the ground, you don't much see the difference. And nowhere else in southern Britain can you find land going cheap as in the Fens. Folks just don't want to live there.

But there's another side too to Lot's scheming. He's in love with Nora, attracted by that tangle of lank black hair that falls whispily over her hawkish features, and doesn't see how the years of injecting heroin have atrophied her features, left her face a knot of burr elm. Likes too the way she lets him stuff his manhood inside her every night, the feeling of sleep that comes over him afterwards. Thick with jealousy, Noah doesn't want other folks' eyes raping his Nora, just 'cause her man's a dimwit and they think they can take advantage. He's searching for a far flung plot out of reach of other men's looks.

It's after dark when they all three crowd into solicitor Blister's office in Ely, Thomas Mobbs a file of documents and maps beneath his arm. And Mr. Blister knows at once the fenman's found a buyer for Forty Foot. He knows too that Thomas Mobbs has been seeking to be rid of this land for over ten years and wonders to his secret self whatever use these dimwits will make of it. Hopes to God they're interested in water sports. Understands the man is half-sharp but sees they're eager to make the purchase and rushes through the affair. He checks over the title-deeds and has a quick look in the land registry then presents the couple with a runic-looking set of title-deeds, a photocopied map of the small-holding's boundaries.

Noah breathes twelve year-old Laphroaig in Nora's hair as she countersigns the cheque that will make them the owners of a tumbledown house, more black silt than they've ever set eyes on and enough water to cause them brain rot.

It's two days later when Noah Lot and Nora return from Ipswich, their Triumph Herald estate car laden to bursting, a roof-rack of scrap metal and a trailer filled with tools. They've got big ideas for their land. Just gotta wait till the water level drops, but Noah's thought it all out and has come prepared. He's got hold of a two-stroke engine and water pump.

It's a hard, sharp, gun-metal type of light, when they turn off the Littleport Road into Forty Foot Lane. The kind of light that foreshadows good weather ushered in after days of rain, Noah thinks. The road is as straight as a knife-cut and is flanked either side by a dyke deep enough to sink a motor. At a steady thirty-five, Noah struggles to hold the wheel of the car that bucks beneath him on the uneven camber corrugated by years of neglect and subsidence. He drops his speed and reasons aloud the road must figure a long way down the Highway Department's repair list. But Noah doesn't care. Rather, he views it as another line in his defence, a deterrent against the unwanted pest of visitors. Takes heart from the field of beet on their left, the brussel sprouts growing on their right. Knows the black fen soil is going to keep them fed.

Two miles further on, the land on their left begins to fall away, the roadside dyke is shored up with a levee on its far side and the buckled surface of tarmac seems to rise steadily above the land like an aeroplane at take-off. The fertile fields give way to floodland and a grey patina of floodwater. Then the road comes to an abrupt right turn, angling off in the direction of Prickwillow, and it's here Noah pulls off the road.

Lot steps out of the car, takes a cigarette from his shirt pocket and lights it. He takes in a deep breath and admires the extent of his floodland that stretches to the dormant snake of the levee of the Forty Foot Drain asleep on the horizon. In between, the expanse of Lot's small-holding, Forty Foot Farm, lies sunk beneath the rippling lake broken only by the silhouette of their farmhouse, rising like an ark through the floodwater. He knows that fourteen inches beneath the surface of the water is the soil from which he's going to make his living, a small patch of the earth's crust which extends in a wedge beneath their feet, as far as the centre of the earth. On the dashboard of the car, the curling pages of a grubby document to prove it. Behind him, in the crook of the Lane's elbow, the land lies higher by a fathom and is ripe with brussels. It's Noah's proof that once the water's shifted off his land he's going to grow a nice crop of vegetables.

"Yoooo!"

His great belly laugh rings out across the water and a moorhen flees to her nest, the ducks take wing. Nora too has got out of the car and is cradling her head on his shoulder.

"D'you think it's going to dry up, Noah?"

"You just wait and see."

"But how do we get to our house? You promised I wouldn't have to swim."

Lot undoes the boot of the car to don the pair of fisherman's waders, the last thing he filched from his father before leaving Ipswich. Doesn't yet realise they're going to be his only useful footwear for the next few months. He is still banking on the fenman's words, remembers how Mobbs said the waters would subside by May and doesn't know that this land has been under a foot of water for the last fifteen years. That he's going to have his work cut out to fix it. He bundles Nora into his forklift arms and balances across the narrow railway-sleeper that spans the dyke - for now the only way of getting to his property - then slides down the bank the other side and begins to slosh his way through the water. It's four hundred yards to the flooded two-up two-down farmstead and by the time he's got two thirds of the way, his arms are beginning to tire. Knows he can't be doing this every day and thinks to himself, until the water level drops, Nora's just going to have to stay indoors.

They arrive at the shoddy pile of brickwork they've invested solid money in, and in the daylight now, see the fist-wide crack cleft in the gable-end, the dearth of slates on the roof. The front door's been washed open by the swell and the ground-floor looks a foot deep in water. He carries

Nora like baggage across the threshold and sets her down on the staircase where she frolics upstairs, willing him to follow her. He plods behind and through the dirty window pane, they look out across the extent of what they've bought. Can see nothing but water and a louring sky. Nora pulls at the top of Noah's waders and wrestles him to the floor. Her lips are wet on his ear and his cock is swelling in his jeans.

The watery sun is impaled on a distant fence-post and the sky turned an inky grey by the time Lot wades back to his car to unload. The Liptons shoppers full of changes of clothing, kitchen-ware, and bedding are going to have to wait till later. His priority's to start shifting water. From his trailer he bundles the paraffin stove, eeling baskets, fishing-rods, grappling hooks and other miscellaneous paraphernalia onto the verge until he uncovers his pump at the bottom. Then hoicks it onto his shoulders and sloshes back toward the levee of the Forty Foot Drain.

Lot's not handsome, the flap of blond hair which falls over the collar of his donkey-jacket, his close-together eyes and tuberose nose all count against him, but there's something admirable in the way he grits himself against adversity. It's getting dark by the time he's finished humping the yards of hoses and tins of two-star to the crown of the levee and it's not easy in the dying light to see how they all connect. But Lot's got hope in his pump. Knows it can shift three hundred gallons an hour and wonders how many gallons are lying on his fields. Doesn't yet know he's underestimated. He's failed to take account of the sponge-like nature of the soil itself and hasn't yet appreciated that unless he also drains the water from the soil beneath, his seeds will rot in the earth. But to Noah, his problem's a simple one: it's just a case of lifting the water off his land and into the Drain. And applies his blunt and stubborn mind to working it out. Looks at it like it's just one of those jobs that needs to be done.

Lot pulls hard on the engine's starter-cord and hears it spluttering to life. He jumps up and down for joy as he sees dirty water sucked up from his land and spewed out into the dyke but doesn't yet know he's going to spend all night, wading through the water every three hours to fill the petrol tank.

To anyone with a knowledge of local geography, Forty Foot Farm is already doomed and the reason fenman Mobbs was anxious to get rid of it, self-evident. Thirty miles inland, Lot's farm lies a good ten feet below sea level. The canal water between the levees of the slow moving Forty Foot, is a bare two feet above the level of the sea and is still several days from the coast. A blockage at Hundred Foot, a rise in levels at the Denver Sluice or a high neap tide in The Wash, will see the dykes back up and burst where they're weakest. And Lot doesn't know that Forty Foot is the more vulnerable to floods than any other farm in East Anglia.

Lot keeps his pump running night and day and after a week sees a drop of half an inch in the water level. Is inclined to attribute it as much to his pump as the drying April wind that's been blowing over the fen. Knows he has to keep the effort up. Each day he takes his five empty gallon tins to the petrol pump at Isleham where he forks out three pounds fifty to refill them. Labours under the mistaken opinion that if he keeps up the effort, with the aid of a long hot summer, he might well get the fen drained.

Meanwhile Nora's getting tetchy. She's been holed up a week now without being able to venture downstairs. There's a limit to the amount of time you can stand at a window in the fens looking out on nothing else but clouds and water. Things are getting boring and the water's beginning to sully her nerves.

"You said it'd be a week and the water'd be gone!" she barks to Lot one lunchtime when he comes in from his wading.

Sitting on the stairs, tugging at his waders, Lot has to scratch his head to find the excuse.

"There's more than what I thought," he meekly proposes.

"And how long d'you expect me to keep banged up here! Haven't seen dry land for a week!"

"Give it another few more days," Lot plays for time, "and you'll see what land we've got."

Nora keeps silent, but Lot gets his answer when he pulls off his waders. There's blotches of green fungi blooming from his feet and he rightly reasons it's his footwear. He knows his feet get sweaty in those waders, and he shouldn't spend all day wearing them, but he can't get around his fen without. It's going to take a while before the water goes down and in the meantime he ought to be making alternative arrangements for getting round his fen. It's the start of a bitter discussion that lasts half the afternoon and the light is fading outside when Lot finally grabs his car keys determined on action.

"I want to come with you," Nora pleads.

Lot's jealous eyes cloud over. He knows there are perverts out there would gladly eye Nora from behind thick-lensed specs, wish that she'd tumble into a barn with them. Is suspicious of the fenmen's morals. Realises he's got to be firm with the girl. If he starts getting soft now, her legs'll end up round a fenman's beard and he'll be using his bullets for more than shooting snipe. He's fighting hard to keep her under his thumb and doesn't dare give an inch now.

"It's a dangerous world in them fen villages. You'll be in trouble if you start venturing out," Lot explains.

"But I only want a ride."

"That's precisely the point," Lot shakes his head at her.

Nora moans something into the wisp of hair falling round her chin, says she knows Lot's right. He's only trying to protect her. Lot says he knows he's right, she ought to listen to him more often. Then storms off across his fen to his car. He's never stolen anything in his life, but there are people in the world better off than himself, and he doesn't see the harm in encouraging a little donation to his cause. Theft, to Noah's gentle mind, would be too strong a word for the felony he's about to commit.

It's almost midnight when Noah returns to Forty Foot with a twelve foot punt he pulled from the river at Grantchester, unaffected by the thought he's just deprived a group of students of their summer recreation. He launches his boat on the ripples of his fen and punts across the water to his house. The reflection of the lamplight from his bedroom window plays on the water and Noah knows Nora's up waiting. He moors his boat by the door and climbs the stairs two at a time still undecided on how he'll break the news. But Nora's sitting strangely silent in the corner and he knows there's something wrong. Sees her gooey smile, and fears for the God-damning worst.

"Wha's up?"

Nora doesn't reply, just smiles an oogley look at Lot, which signals the flare about to burst.

"He were only visiting," Nora smiles back in a fey voice.
"Who was?"

"Mobbs. Thomas Mobbs. To see if we was alright."

"You mean he set foot on my property…!"

It's the start of an all night argument, as Lot sees in his mind, his woman ravished by an ugly fenman. Can't believe Nora's protests that the visit was purely civil. No amorous intentions were ever aired and she never let him upstairs. But it's all too much for Lot's jealous temperament. He rages all night and swears revenge on Mobbs until sometime towards dawn, Nora finally plays host to his manhood and promises it's been the first occasion of the night.

Nevertheless, Lot's not going to take chances. The next morning, words thick in anguish, and wishing he had the ammunition to hurl a more direct blow at fenman Mobbs, Noah paints the notice which he'll later display at the elbow of the Forty Foot Lane. Wants the public to get the message that he isn't going to share his Nora among them and isn't going to have the fenmen issue his bastards, either. Then punts across his fen to post his ultimatum:

```
ИOAH LOT
FOURTY FOOT FARM
KEEPOUT
```

And spends the rest of the morning punting Nora round the fen, giving her a tour of his plans.

Nora likes the new means of transport, finds it preferable to wading but as she has to tell him, he's building castles on water unless he gets the fen drained first.

Lot has to concede that Nora's right. The water is the source of their problems, and it's not going down as fast as he'd envisaged. For the first three weeks up the fen, they've eaten little but eels and it's now playing havoc with his stomach. He can't say he ever had any great passion for the taste of these unctuous fen-worms which in any case are difficult to catch, but for the last four days he's had cramps in his gut that he can only put down to his diet. He's longing for the day when the water level drops and he's able to grow a few vegetables.

But gut-rot is not his only motivation. Hounded by insomnia, he's begun to have nightmares of dam-bursts, flood-water breaching the levees of the Forty Foot. His pump's not as powerful as he'd hoped and he knows that if they ever have a problem with the levee, his pump will be next to useless. He's known for a while, that he can't keep frittering his money on two-star, that the daily trips to

Isleham are becoming expensive. But he's damned if he can find a solution.

Until, that is, the night in late April when he lies awake in his bed, listening to the gale howling outside and rattling the slates on his roof. Wonders why nature should be so disruptive to the lives of people, then is hit by a brainwave at precisely the time he hears the bricks come tumbling from his chimney. Says to Nora snoring beside him, "There's a lot of weather here. We ought to put it to use."

Insomniac Noah once again resorts to cruising the local area in his Triumph Herald. This time, the ex-apprentice panel-beater unwise in agriculture, half-wise in engineering is on a tour of the fenland rubbish skips and dumping grounds. He's collecting old tractor gearboxes, pneumatic piston cases, drive-shafts, transmission units, wheels, cogs and cams. It all goes in his trailer to be taken back to Forty Foot where his spare bedroom is becoming so well stocked in scrap metal that the joists are threatening to give way beneath it. Nora can't understand why on earth she has to wrestle with big ends and suspension units just to get to her linen basket. But Noah's mind is not easy to understand. It turns by a logic of which other folk just don't possess.

Noah now passes daytimes in his shed, water sloshing round his feet, his toes getting cold in the end of his waders, hammering at bits of metal, going upstairs only for a lunch when Nora calls down that the eel stew or roast coot is ready. With a hacksaw and metal punch he's bashing at a sheet of aluminium, trying to forge the shape of a wind-rose. It gets a little lonely working on his own all day, but he knows he hasn't the choice if he's going to get the water shifted. Wishes he had a friend to keep him company or that Nora would take an interest in socket-spanners, but knows it's not the case. Hits on the solution of keeping sane by telling himself jokes, reminding himself of the days when he was young.

For three weeks, Lot machines away with his rudimentary tools, little more than a rasp, hammer and hand-drill, towards the completion of his windpump. It's a chill night in early May when Lot stays up all night machining the final touches to a cam shaft to complete his windpump and after a breakfast of brackish tea and moorhen, he lugs the results of his patient engineering to the Drain. On the crest of the levee he's already got four scaffold poles, once belonging to a Swaffham builder, driven into the soil at each corner of a two-foot square. Lot works without a break all day, his actions slurred by loss of sleep and his brain numbed by the chill breeze blowing off the fen but by late afternoon, an eight-bladed wind-rose, four feet in diameter, beaten from a solid sheet of aluminium, turns on a trunnion at the summit of his column, bright metal flashing in the evening sun. The longitudinal fin balanced behind it keeps it keen to the wind, and Lot sees how it mirrors every nuance in the wind's changing directions. He disengages the clutch. A multi-directional gear transforms the wind's power down a vertical drive-shaft to a journal box where a crank wheel drives a shuttle-action piston. The pump is a Victorian water pump he borrowed from the village green at Histon late one night and he grins with happiness as he sees it disgorging the fen-water into the dyke. For the larger part of an hour Lot stands mesmerised by his creation, this near humanoid shape which is doing the work of his two-stroke without costing him a penny. Reckons it a thing of great beauty and genius. A pump that works purely by the weather.

The wind is only moderate but, against his wristwatch, he times the pump to be running at twenty three cycles a minute. He's reckoned the pump's capacity at around four pints. Arithmetic's not easy for Noah, but later that night, with Nora's help and a long calculation later, he's worked out his new pump moves over seven hundred gallons an hour. He laughs out loud with joy, thinks his creation deserves a bit of celebration and suggests to Nora she might like to share it.

Lot's lonely head, short on language, long on mechanics is gradually turning things round. The weather that summer is kind to Lot and the projects burning in his slow-fused mind are quick in being realised. He's proving to the fen folk how the soil should be managed, displays an intuitive flair that would have challenged even Newton or Vermuyden. Gets on with his life with a contempt for the rest of humanity that is almost admirable.

Lot's not clever, but pitting his mind against water, he's able to come up with solutions. Has hit upon the idea that what he needs on his fen is something that drinks a lot of water and for the last few weeks he's been looking around for a thirsty beast. Still hounded by his cursed insomnia, he's been driving out each night to Swaffham, Downham, Thetford. He's been coming back at dawn, exhausted from a night of digging and a trailer full of willow saplings, which he plants round his fen. Setting them round the perimeters of large square plots, he's using them to mark out the boundaries of his future fields. Knows nothing of transpiration, hasn't a clue what happens to it all, but has the stubborn idea that a few dozen willows planted out round his fen are going to drink up all this water. Is not so very far from the truth.

By the end of May, the water's down to six inches. It makes sploshing around on his property all the easier. He's abandoned his waders now for a pair of wellingtons and his punt is reserved only for the deepest waterways. He's constructed a bridge over the dyke and with care he can drive his car across the bridge and through the water to the front door of his house. A load of hard-core dumped by his doorstep enables him to park above the level of the water. The eight inch drop in the water level since they first arrived in March has meant he's now got two clear acres of land around the perimeter of his small-holding. Planted out on that ribbon of land he's got carrots, celery, turnips and brussels sprouts. Can already see the day when there's a change in the menu from eating eel soup and moorhen stew.

It's a blustery early June evening when Lot comes in from surveying his lake that Nora serves up the dish of eel soup and scurvy tea which they eat in habitual silence. It's nearly three months now they've been up the farm and Nora hasn't once been off the fen. She tidies away the plates, gives him a cute kind of smile and Noah sees it as the moment to pitch his suggestion:

"Being as it's Friday, how about a half pint of shandy in Isleham?"

"But, like you said, Noah, it's dangerous for me down the village."

"I'm not asking you to go alone. I'll make sure folks don't look at you."

Unconvinced, Nora just hunches her shoulders and gives Noah a squirmy kind of look.

"Maybe another night."

Slowly things have changed inside Nora's head. She's glad now for the solitude of Forty Foot Farm. Doesn't think she could stand the crowd that gathers in a pub. Years of injecting heroin in her arm, living in a squat in Ipswich, taught her the world's not a pretty place and the worst of it is undoubtedly people. She's thankful to Lot for having saved her from the torment of other people's company. Can't see why she has to go and mix with people now. Is content with the company of moorhens and coots that swim by her window.

Two weeks later, Nora finds she's missed a period. Tells Noah she thinks she ought to see a doctor, but doesn't want to go into town. Asks if he can't call a doctor. Lot has visions of a fen doctor staring up between her legs and knows he has to put the lid on the idea.

"Ugh. Doctor and mid-husband is me here."

Nora, poor broken soul, doesn't dare insist.

"Think she'll be a boy?"

Lot puts his hand on her belly and grunts. He hasn't got a clue about children.

~

By late autumn, Noah's got the Forty Foot Drain cleared of the sedges that were choking it and now sees the water move unimpeded to The Wash. He's dug a good set of trenches to convey the water from the distant corners of his plot to the three windpumps now up and running and there's hardly a puddle on his land. He's got a good dozen willows round his farm, all drawing water from their roots and his petrol-driven pump has been demoted to reserve. The house is shored up with scaffolding so as the turf shrinks beneath it won't topple, and he's filled the cleft in the gable-end. Where the soil is already well-drained there are two acres of turnips and a half-acre of sprouts. Elsewhere he's got leeks, carrots, cabbages, beet, and once a week, Lot takes his surplus crop to sell on the market in King's Lynn. The returns aren't great, but he can't see how else he's going to make any money and it's enough at least to buy next year's seed. Can already see the day when he'll be able to start keeping stock and make the next move towards self-sufficiency.

But late-October sees a deluge pouring from the sky. It hasn't stopped raining for three days now and Noah's been watching Forty Foot rising steadily. It's seventy-two hours he hasn't slept a moment but has been pacing the levee, racking his brains as to how to stop the levee bursting. Noah stops his pumps, knows there's no point in pumping water into an already over-flowing Drain. Better let it lie upon the land.

He's always reckoned that the water in Forty Foot moves at a stroll's pace, but now he's sure the water's slowing up. Then at dusk on the third day he sees the flow of water in his Drain come to a halt and knows it's no longer going anywhere. Except rising. He begins to panic, wonders what earthly forces can conspire to stop a river and knows the situation is serious. But when, an hour later, he observes the river going into reverse, he understands the water's flowing in from the sea. And his only explanation is the world's begun to tip. Is no longer the vast level fen that he supposes, but some kinky bevel come to plague him.

Noah throws himself into a rage, sees the months of hard work washed away if he doesn't do something quick. He calls out to Nora asleep in her bunk, tells her the world's tipping up and she has to come and help him stop it. Noah has no reserve of sandbags to hold down the earth. But the two of them shovel soil onto a barrow and carry it to the levee where their pitiful effort of trying to heighten the levee is fast in vain.

For twelve hours Noah works like a madman. At dawn, it gets critical, a trickle of water begins to flow over the lip of the bank. As fast as they stop it, they see another trickle elsewhere. Noah knows he shouldn't do it, but there's no other choice. Grabbing a pick-axe in his terror-raging hands, he jumps into the Drain and swims the dozen yards to the far side. Dragging himself onto the far bank he raises the pick above his shoulders and hefts a scupper in the turf. Gladly sees the Drain disgorge its water on the adjoining farmland.

What Noah doesn't know, however, is the thing that's going to save them has already happened.

Midday the previous day was high tide in The Wash and the water authorities had no choice but to close the Denver Sluice. It was that which caused the water in the fen drains to back up and the water levels to rise - a small risk compared to the danger threatened by the tide. With low tide at midnight, they'd opened the sluice and the waters in the dykes had already begun to shift. At dawn, Noah sees the level in the Forty Foot Drain begin to drop. And the rain too is already letting up.

Lot survived the high neap tide in the Wash, but he still has to get through the winter. After five o'clock it's too dark to be out on his fen and with Nora no longer in the condition to contain his libido, he's at a loss for entertainment in the evening. While Nora snores away her pregnancy upstairs, Lot takes to staring into the flames of the fire and amusing himself telling stories. Most of them are tales of his adventures on the fen and few of them would hold a friend's attention, but they're the only stories Lot knows. He laughs out loud at their unfunny endings and jibes at his own innuendoes. Then it's one night Nora awakes to hear a whole party going on downstairs and realises it's only Noah jabbering away to himself. She dons her woolly jumper and creeps downstairs. She puts her head round the door to see Lot rocking in his chair cackling away at his own jokes.

"Noah?"

Lot leaps with terror as if a fen-monster has just risen from the dyke.

"Noah! Who have you been talking to?"

His imaginary world now cracked open, Lot begins to leap around the room.

"Nothing. It isn't nothing I was saying. Just listening."

"Noah! You've been talking for over an hour! What have you been saying? Who d'you imagine you've been talking to?"

"It's nothing, honest. Just stories."

But Nora looks at him through woolly eyes. She can tell by the way Noah is now crouching in the corner that something's not right. She cuts a blow through the air with her words.

"Noah, you've been talking to yourself."

"I haven't."

But Noah's denial masks the slow awareness he's no longer in control of his mind. And as Nora turns to head upstairs to bed, Noah crouches down before the fire and realises he's got to find something better to do with his time. He crawls up the stairs an hour later, thinking he might have hit on the solution.

The next morning finds him experimenting with alcohol. He's up early to go and buy the pack of brewer's yeast from the chemist's in Littleport. By mid-morning, he's taken control of the kitchen with the four bags of sugar, plastic dustbin and large sack of turnips. There's nothing involved about the way he mashes up his turnips and strains their juice through an old cotton vest into the dustbin below, then adds to the murky concoction, sugar, yeast and two gallons of fen water, before he leaves it in the corner to ferment .

Two weeks later, Lot tastes his first brew of turnip wine and declares it a passable tipple. It's not strong but it's good for slaking his thirst and after the year or so of abstinence from drinking, he doesn't need much before the feeling of sleep washes over him. He no longer jabbers to himself in the dead of night and Nora concludes he might have found a way of putting the cork on the bottle of his incipient madness.

From this day on, after the fashion of his biblical name-sake, Noah Lot embarks on the recreation of a sot. He still works harder then ten men put together all day, but the minute the sun sets and his draining and ditching work is done for the day he begins an evening of remarkable drinking. Drinks to get drunk, to keep the fen at bay and does a remarkable good job of it.

It's late March when Nora suffers the most terrible labour. Lot lays her out on the ground floor of the cottage, sees the pain she's in and thinks she's going to die. But can't call a doctor now. They'd wonder why he's left it so late. He takes a blunt knife from the kitchen and thinks he'd better make a few small cuts. Sees Nora screaming with pain and decides against it. Believes it's a mater of brute force. Takes the small head in his hands and pulls with all his might till Nora sees what he's doing to the child and starts to scream out louder.

Half an hour later a boy gets born and Lot decides to call his son Ig. Can't be bothered with a long name with too many letters. Two is all he can spare. Besides, considering how many times he's going to have to use it, he might as well save himself some energy.

After the birth of her son, Nora is more content to be con-fined indoors. She spends her time looking after the boy and is pleased to have herself company that makes a change from Lot's bluntness. She's never thought of herself as a mother until now, but with something to coddle she reckons she's found her vocation. She can't remember any of the nursery-rhymes her mother taught her, but in the afternoon, when Ig lies swaddled in its cot, she sings to it eely lullabies which she makes up herself.

A tinge of nostalgia overtakes Nora. She's proud of her boy and she'd like to take it to her ageing mother in Ipswich. She'd be proud to think she's a granny. Ig is lying in his cot one afternoon when Noah comes in from eeling and Nora broaches the subject.

"Noah, d'you think we shouldn't ought to make a last visit to Ipswich. Take Ig to see his grandparents?"

A storm blows up in Noah's head. He hasn't thought about his parents for over a year now, and he thought Nora had forgotten about hers too. What do they want with parents at this time in their lives? They'd only want to come and visit the farm. Then they'd start coming every weekend and before he knew it, the floodgates would've opened and every Harry, Dick and Tim would be up there.

"Nora." Lot shakes his head.

"What?"

"Both our parents died long ago. Don't you remember?"

"Did they? What? My Mum and Dad? They're dead?"

"You've even forgotten."

"Oh, Noah." And Nora, breaks down in tears on Lot's shoulder. Lot, guilty now that his lie has been swallowed so easily, massages Nora's shoulders in a way that he hasn't done for over a year. Thinks to himself, she's getting vulnerable, fragile, living up here. But is certain now there's no chance she'd go running off with a fenman. Nora sobs into his chest and pulls him down onto the kitchen floor with a hunger she hasn't had for months. They're at it all after-noon and Ig's crying from his cot goes ignored.

And ten months later, Ug gets born. A monster of a boy whose entrance into the world causes Nora more pain even than she suffered with Ig.

The pain of Ug's birth is also the birth of the pictures in Nora's head which, with the passing of the years, have be-come ever more frequent. Daytimes, Noah is out on his fen, clearing his Dyke of sedges, tilling his loam or harvesting vegetables, returning to the house at lunch time only for long enough to down a pint of eel stew before returning to the solitude of his fen and in the evening, after his meal, he sits in his chair by the fire, dedicating himself to turnip wine and snoring. Hounded by loneliness, racked by confu-sion and convinced that something is tooling away at her mind, Nora has turned in on herself.

One morning, staring out at the fen from the kitchen window, a tune from long ago starts playing through her mind and a fragmented lyric, like a record-player stuck in a groove, starts swirling in her head. She tries to bring to mind the four musicians' names but can't get further than The Beatles. Knows her head's all messed up. Is too full of pictures, images that clog it all up. Words are slipping from her mind. No longer used they are soon forgotten. And in their place are forming the stalactite crusts of hallucina-tions, incubi, pictures, crowding her mind like fen-demons.

It's only night times, when the Lot family are all crowded into the same large pile of bedding on the floor that Nora feels comfort. She's got Noah snuggled beside her, whispering in her ear his grunts and groans, thick in onomatopoeia, before he rolls on top of her and puts her to sleep.

It's one night though, when the fen outside is quiet as sprouting corn, and Noah thumps away on top of her and Nora becomes aware of the far end of the blanket moving in a wave. She knows this is not a picture in her head. She pushes Noah's steaming body away from her and gives her boys a wallop so hard they don't fall asleep till dawn from all the tears they shed.

Ig and Ug are growing up fast, and Nora knows they're short on language, vitamins, and basic knowledge and thinks they ought to go to school. Tells Noah the next morning over breakfast, she's not going to tolerate her sons' behaviour, says it's time they went to school. The patriarch scowls back like she's just gone out of her fen.

"It's people, Nora. They're no good for you. Send those kids to school and they get ideas funny. It's other people, see. They fuck you up bad. Better stay here on Noah's fen." Noah chases the boiled moorhen's egg round his plate, then spears it with his fork and swallows it. He's been in a foul temper the last few mornings, hasn't been sleeping well at night and knows his sleeping draught of turnip wine is no longer acting as it should. For several days now he's been resolved on doing something about it.

"My boys got a fen to learn them. Know the words for vegetables, nature and tools. What my boys do with other more 'ophisticated words, like "ditcation", "mulpitlication" an' all that crap from school? Better stay here on Noah's fen. Getting good at machines. Ig already show me other day what he mend a puncture. Clever. Ig too clever for go school."

Nora slaps down a mug of hip tea and brushes the hair away from round her face. Noah is still punishing the eggs on his plate then he looks up and adds his final word.

"Besides. Those boys got work do. Gotta help out father Noah."

Then he gets up from the table and lurches out of the kitchen determined on work.

He dedicates a morning boiling a tin of turnip wine over a burner in his shed where a crude wrangle of pipes carry the steam to a slowly filling wine-bottle. Little technology is applied to his method and Noah understands nothing of methyl and ethyl, he's just following some vague recollection of the way to make whisky. He doesn't want to waste his turnip wine, but he knows he's got to find a way to make it stronger, something that will put him in his loft at nights. Sees his salvation in alcohol and bends down to turn up the flame on his paraffin stove. A taut morning later, nerves all a-jitter, Noah has a bottleful of hooch. He pours himself a glass and sips the clear liquid, a sharp wood alcohol, sparkling as water. Immediately, he totters on his feet and knows he's found the answer to his sleepless nights and his recently sagging libido.

It's two months later Lot gets a visit from the social services. A girl in a Ford Escort pulls up at the farm and Lot senses bother the minute she steps out of the car with a clipboard in hand and high heels on her feet. Knows straight away she hasn't come to ask about the price of cabbage and knows there's trouble in her visit. It's a hot June morning and the fen gleams before them, a plate of luscious vegetables, a grebe crying out from its nest on the dyke.

"So what you come to tell me, love?"

"According to our records at Town Hall, Mr. Lot. you've got a son approaching school-going age."

Lot wonders how the hell she ever got to hear about the life of son Ig but he's unaware of the gossip that circulates round Littleport about the family of idiots that live up on Forty Foot. He leans more heavily on the bonnet of her car and eyes her through the fatty pouches of skin that are threatening to envelope his eyes. The girl senses violence in Noah Lot's stare and backs away.

"None of my childs are going school, you understand? They learn up here at Forty Foot. Father Noah as headmaster."

"But you know Mr. Lot, the law requires all children of school-going age to be educated. If you're not going to send your boy to school, we'll want to see what provision you're making."

Lot shows her the extent of his fen. Says what does a boy need to read for if he's got all this to look after, and the girl from social services jots his reply down in her notebook. Sorely wonders too if any of the children have ever seen a doctor, have had the inoculations and what they eat for dinner. Sees them growing up on a diet of turnips and brussel sprouts. Is not so far from the truth.

"And has he had his inoculations?"

The lid begins to lift off Lot's temper. He can't see why she has to come interfering in their lives like this. It's his boy after all and he can bring him up how he likes. Wants to give the girl a slice of his opinion.

"'Nocerlations? What the hell my boys want them for? How the hell they gonna catch malaria up here? You wanna go 'n' get your facts sorted, love."

But the girl isn't finished yet. Says she needs to have a quiet word with Ig.

Mr. Lot calls out to his son to stop fishing for eels in the ditch and come and speak to the lady from the council.

Ig, face a star-map of freckles and raffia fringe leaps from the ditch pointing his eeling pike like an offensive weapon at the woman.

"Now put that down, come over here," she asserts. "Now, tell me what your name is."

Ig looks at his father all cross-eyed. Doesn't understand when someone's addressing him. And the girl from the social is of a mind to press on with her questioning.

"Now. Ig. You are Ig, aren't you? Now, would you like to go to school?"

"Yaaah!" Ig heaves his eel pike into the air like a javelin and charges off back to his ditch of eels.

He just confirmed to the girl that loonies beget loonies, that the boy is out of control already, and to put him in a school would cause serious disruption to the other pupils' learning. She reasons that the best they can do is leave this family alone on the fen and hope they don't do anyone any harm. She thanks Lot for the interview, gets back in her Escort and heads back to Town Hall, mindful that the only useful act would be to bin the folder on the Lot family and pretend they don't exist.

It's the last the social services ever bother Lot. And the Town Hall is destined to remain ignorant of the blood that's boiling up at Forty Foot.

Ten years pass. Noah's got Forty Foot more or less sorted and to most intents and purposes the farm's self sufficient. He's got thirty acres down to root crops, vegetables, and a dozen or so over to livestock and fowl. The days of eel soup are all but memories and he can bring up his children on a healthy diet. He still puts in his share of the labour, but his two elder sons Ig and Ug do a lot to help him now. It's over a year since he's been into Littleport, perhaps a couple since he set foot in Ely, and he can't remember the last time he went to Downham. Long gone are the days when he used to pedle his sacks of sprouts and boxes of carrots on the stalls of local markets. He hasn't the need now for the extra cash and besides, his Triumph Herald's rusted out and he's chocked it up on blocks as a hen coop. He's happy up here on his fen. Doesn't have to bother with other people and he can just get on with living his life. He's proud too of his achievement. For a dimwit, it's not a bad estate.

There are five littluns now. Besides Ig and Ug, there's Og, ten, and Eg and Ag, the twins, eight. Lot deems them happy. Or at least they should be. They've got a horizon all to themselves, more playing fields than most other kids their age and they don't have to go to school.

As her children grow older and her husband sinks deeper into his inebriate shell, mother Nora is the one now left on her own. She hasn't been off Forty Foot Fen for fifteen years and she's forgotten there's a world out there. Late in the evening, unable to sleep, she wanders the fen alone, calling out like some berserk Norsewoman to an unknown, long-forgotten, Scandinavian God. And the villagers in Little-port, four miles off, taking their dogs out for walks in the long summer air, hear the howls of a madwoman which add fuel to their rumours of Forty Foot.

Ig's now fifteen and he's taken after father Noah. He's got the same haddock face, a cob of blond hair that hangs round his shoulders and those same starey eyes that once frightened the girl from social services. Most of the time he's out on the fen managing the flow of water through the ditches or its vertical journey through the pumps to the Drain, or tending to his crops of sprouts or turnips. He's got a good feel for agriculture and under his direction, the yield of Forty Foot has doubled in the last two years. In the evenings after dinner, while Noah's asleep in his metaphorical tree, Ig sulks out to his father's shed where he dedicates himself to engineering and science. He's taught himself mechanics by patient years of dismantling engines, gear boxes, pneumatic piston cases with a spanner and he's applied his knowledge to the fen, found ways of harnessing the power of his windmills and heaven knows where from, he's learnt about electric too. He's got a generator running off a windpump that brings light to the house in the evenings.

He's never been to school and, save for his one visit from social services, has never spoken to anyone outside his family. Doesn't know what conversation is. He's never had need of it anyway. There's never been anyone to talk to. Knows there's other people in the world, but doesn't know that folks can be talked to.

There's something else too that burns away in Ig's mind. Something he lacks the words to express. A childhood of hoeing and ditching and a diet of waterfowl and eels have given Ig muscles but his jerky movements hide an inner rage, as if something inside him is left insatiate. He's never seen a girl in his life except his sister Ug. Knows all about the workings of a woman's valves, but has never put it to the test. Has no idea of feelings. Knows it feels good when they're all huddled up in bed at night and remembers the enjoyment his father used to get from mounting his mother. But has no idea how to make sense of it all. Lets it all jumble around in his head like marbles in a jar.

It's a wet March afternoon when Noah's asleep in his tree, Ig's brothers and sister are all out on the fen and mother Nora is working in the kitchen preparing a duck for the oven. Ig appears at the door, his hand on his fly and speaking in oily grunts. When Nora turns, she sees a look in Ig's eyes like she's never seen before and knows that the boy means damage. She flies into a rage and begins to belt him with a cloth. Ig can't understand what's gone wrong. Begins to thrash out at his mother and at last he grabs her by the throat. Nora screams for him to let go but Ig is incensed and in the flailing that follows, his fist knocks his mother's jaw. He hears the bone crack and his mother screaming out in pain. Sees her limp jaw hanging loose from her face and knows that when his father sets eyes on it, it will be the end. Ig scarpers from the house and begins to run. He has no idea where he's going, just knows he's got to get away. He arrives at the Drain and swims across. Splashing through the sedges, he can already hear his father hollering from the house and knows he has to get sprinting. Limp with fear, he hauls himself out of the drain and sets off across the fen without a clue where he's going. He's never in his life set foot off Forty Foot.

For five days Ig's wandering the fen catching eels with his bare hands and eating them raw, scrumping sprouts, cabbages, carrots from the fields and drinking ditch water, unaware of the Hell that's going on back at Forty Foot.

Then it's one evening he winds up in Ely. He's never seen so many houses so close together before and wonders at the thought of it all. Can't conceive of life without a field of sprouts and is amazed by streetlights, road traffic and the enormous castle. But he knows he's not a pretty sight and doesn't want anyone to see him. He doesn't know where he's going but after five days of camping out in ditches there's a longing to find somewhere dry. He heads through an archway, pads along a narrow path and sees a small shade of trees to his right. Knows he could camp the night there.

He's just curled up, trying to get some sleep when the sound of footsteps on the pavement wakes him. He has no-idea it's just past closing time and the pubs have disgorged their drinkers out into the night air. He looks out from the cover of his wood and sees something like sister Ug, but nicer, threading a languid path towards him. Fifteen feet from his eyes, she stops to search in her handbag for a ciga-rette. She's swaying like father Noah after his turnip liquor, and she sits down on a bench to smoke, then takes some-thing from her bag, holds it to her ear and starts to talk. She's cackling away and Ig gets the idea she's talking to him, feels the manhood in his trousers stiffen and under-stands she's the thing he's wanted all his life.

He jumps out of the wood and flings his arms around her. He drags her to his hideout in the trees and begins to wrestle her. But she's shouting out loud and making a noise and Ig knows he somehow has to stop her and holds his hands down on her neck, till she stops making all that racket. Then begins to unbutton his trousers. Ten minutes later, he leaves her lifeless corpse on the ground and flees into the fens.

Ig's asleep in a ditch near Manea when, five days later, the police find the crazed fen idiot. He feels the cold metal of the shackles round his wrist and awakes to find himself surrounded by men in fluorescent yellow jackets bundling him into a van with a flashing blue light. Hasn't got a clue what's going on. Or why they're treating him so badly.

But nor does Ig know the other story either.

When the woman's body is found on the common the fol-lowing morning, the police know at once it's a member of the Forty Foot family. Only one of them would leave moorhen feathers at the scene of a murder. They dispatch a car up to Forty Foot Fen to interview Noah.

The two officers later speak of a family of cowards who flee into the hiding of their house the moment their Rover turns down the drive. Only patriarch Noah, dishevelled and scattered, is brave enough to face them. He stands guard at the entrance to his shed with an eeling pike which he only lowers when he sees the police have not come to harm him. There's little sense in the man's talk, but they persuade him they need to have a word. Seeing the visitors have not come to hurt them, Noah's family emerge from their hiding holes. First to venture out is Nora, a length of cloth wrapped round her head, strapping her jaw to her head, then, one by one, the reticent gamins who speak a dialect of English almost unrecognisable. The police don't understand a word and turn to interrogate Lot.

"Mr. Lot, we'd like to speak to your son Ig."

"You finded Ig?"

The police don't reply.

"You finded Ig, you keep him. Noah don't want him no more. Ig he broked my Nora's head. Ig he gone away far. Not come back here, no more Ig. No more Noah's son Ig."

Noah spares them the details of his son's assault, but he's already confirmed the police officers' suspicions.

"No, Mr. Lot, we haven't got your son Ig. But we would like to talk to him. So if he does come back, I wonder if you would be so kind as to get in touch with us?"

"What Ig done?"

"We don't know that Ig's done anything yet, but we'd like to talk to him all the same."

"What you want talk about? Father Noah tell you."

"We just want to talk to him at this stage Mr. Lot. I'm afraid we can't yet tell you what it's in connection with but I trust you'll co-operate over the matter. And in the meantime, hope Mrs. Lot's jaw gets better"

As one of the officers will later testify, as they turn to get into their car, they see Noah Lot turn as white as a fen ghost. Like a premonition has just hit him on the head.

Noah Lot's worked all his adult life to turn round Forty Foot. And he's done his damn near best to bring his children up well. He's kept them from evil. And people. Stuck to his motto. But the visit from the police has made him worry. Ig's already turned his temper beyond forgiveness, but if the police want to talk to him, it means he's gone and done something nasty. And if Ig's in trouble with the law, Noah reasons, it's the whole Lot family will go down in Littleport's history as a family of criminals. And Noah can't bear the weight of accusation.

That night Lot drinks more than his usual draught of turnip hooch and sits staring into the fire, jabbering on about when times were good. It's always the same. People. Can't escape them. Not even up here on Forty Foot. Always kept his kids away from other people but he'll be damned if the first time they do they get themselves into trouble. It's always bloody other people that make them do wrong. That's what happens when you go mixing with folks. Evil. And Lot knows the police aren't going to leave them alone now. They'll keep coming back. And Lot could tell one of them had eyes for Nora. It's gonna end bad for the Lots.

They were yet to find Ig asleep in the ditch at Manea when the same pair of officers called again on Forty Foot two days later. This time there was no Noah to salute them with an eel pike, but instead, what PC Woolwich and WPC Parratt discovered, shocked them into a month of sick leave.

In each of the six willow trees around Lot's farm, a body was hanging from the branches, a few yards from each, a kicked-away milk crate. And the only explanation, suicide. Noah Lot's family, in a gesture of madness, solidarity, despair, (which, we'll never know) hanged themselves from trees in the slow March sun.

Thomas
Mumford

Thomas Mumford had struggled all his life to make ends meet, had always been short of a coin, but now, in the twilight of his years, he found it harder to get by than ever. After the ounce of Golden Virginia, the thirteen shillings rent each week on his cottage and three halves of brown ale each night in the Green Man, he had just enough left over to put a crust of bread between his dentures before he went to bed. Or so he always told us, and looking at the man, as lean as cat-meat, face like a sparrow-hawk, there was no reason to go disbelieving him. He got his eggs from the farm, kept an enviable kitchen-garden, and fetched the odd rabbit from the hedgerow when he could, but there was no spare cash in the Mumford coffers to go paying for things like Council Tax. Not even if they took back his medals from the war or turned him upside down to shake the life-long patriotism from his heart and to see what fell from his pockets. He'd lived an honest life and couldn't see why the country he'd served as lance-corporal Mumford should see fit to betray him now.

It was one Sunday evening, a month before the last general elections when the gaunt-figured septuagenarian sat in the Green Man, half of brown ale cupped between his palms, resolutely speaking thus.

In his day he'd laid a hedge the way a weaver worked the loom, made a hedgerow into art, turned a scraggy no-hoper, thick with elder, short in thorn into a sheep-tight fold. He could sort the bramble from the rose, weave a wicket from hazel, and tell the age of any hedge just by casting his eye at its mix of species. With only his old dog Bodger for company, hatchet grasped by frost-chapped fingers, back turned against the wind, he'd hacked his way through the cold winter months, grubbing out the dead-wood, selecting the saplings he would leave for standards, and laid his pleachers like they were plaits in a maiden's hair, binding them tight with withy. Then at the end of the day, eyes smarting from wood-smoke, young Thomas Mumford would bury his foil-wrapped tatties in the embers of his fire, wrap his hatchet in sack-cloth and point his bi-cycle home-bound, faithful dog Bodger following behind him at a trot. In the summers, when the sap was up in the hedgerows, and there was no hedging work to be had, he took to doing piece-work on Handley's farm, working the binder, feeding the threshing drum, or in later years, keep-ing it all running smooth in the grain-drier.

Now at seventy-seven, he was stooped like a bill-hook from long Decembers bent double against the wind and sultry Augusts standing stooks in the wheat-field. He always wore a waistcoat, or 'wescot' as he called it, hung over those arching, scythe-like shoulders and indoors or out, the same flat-cap was always pressed down hard on the crown of his head. Sipping the warm, wet beer in the Green Man, face a rage of purple, he would every now and then dip his hand into his waistcoat pocket to take out a wild horse-radish root which he dug up from along the railway embankment.

Said a nibble on that was better than snuff for clearing the nose.

Born two summers after the end of the Great War, he'd lived all his life in Buckworth and knew every hedge in Huntingdonshire, so he said. As a young man at the end of the forties, just back from widow-making and glad not to be widow's husband himself, he had done well for himself, had more work than his time allowed for and was taking all the prizes at the county shows. But Tom Mumford never had a head for finance. Didn't have the heart, they always said, to charge his full worth and always underpriced his labour. When folks in the village were telling him he ought to be saving his stamps for his pension he never gave it a thought. Said the future was a long way off and before it arrived something else was bound to come along.

Only once, they rumoured, he'd been in love and it had scarred his heart for life. It was long before I arrived in the village and I heard about it only later from what other people told me, but gossip being the way it is, the story's probably truer than the facts. The year he came back from the war, twenty-six year old lance-corporal Mumford discovered the lion in his breeches that the Tunisian desert and years of homesickness had kept caged up so long. It was the daughter of an American fireman stationed on the air-base who courted his leonine appurtenance and before young Thomas Mumford could catch his breath, he'd lost his heart and his cherries all in one. For a couple of summers he was hardly fit to carry to work, so drawn out he was from cycling back at dawn from his trysts in Houghton meadows. The wedding was announced and the banns read in Houghton church. All the girls in Buckworth raged with jealousy for the flounce-frocked Beverly Summers, mouthful of American, face full of freckles, now engaged to their sweetheart Tom. Then two months before the wedding, fireman Summers got a sudden posting back to Arizona and the marriage was postponed until Tom could come out to the States to join her. Never were more tears shed than on young Beverly's departure but if all went well, Tom would have saved up enough for his passage within the twelve-month and they'd be having an American honeymoon. For six months he worked like a dog trying to save up the coppers to join his sweetheart away in Arizona and Beverly was writing every week wondering when he was going to join her, saying she couldn't wait much longer. After a year he'd saved up half the fare and he wrote her a letter to say if she'd just hang on another twelve months he'd be with her. But Tom never saw the end of that year. A few months later he received a Dear John, said she hadn't been able to wait that long and had found another sweetheart, was engaged to be married, knew Tom would be broken-hearted by the news, but thought it best to tell him straight.

They say Thomas Mumford never got over the despair and took to reading books, lost himself among the words of Hemingway and Henry David Thoreau, searched for consolation in the poems of Walt Whitman. He read everything on America he could ever get his hands on, and they said in those days you were as likely to see him standing by a shelf of books in Huntingdon library as you would beside a hedge, as if Beverly Summers' heart was to be found among all those words. For three years, they say he almost gave up working, fed himself on reading and broken dreams, promising himself he'd get there one day, see if Beverly might change her mind.

He never lost that passion for the States and if you hadn't known about his sweetheart Beverly, you'd have thought it strange why an English Hodge would sit in the Green Man of an evening quoting lines of Thomas Jefferson, Abraham Lincoln, Steinbeck. Talked of America like it was his own second home, said he'd be going back there soon.

Then in the fifties, just as he began to emerge from his loneliness once more, things got hard for a hedge-laying man because of what was going on in the East of England. The land all went over to arable and there was no more need for stock-tight hedgerows, no one cared for hedge-layers any more and all of a sudden work was hard to come by. He had to travel into Northamptonshire to pick up jobs and had to run a van and lay out costs for petrol. Later still, with the coming of the combines, farmers found small fields uneconomical and ripped up the hedgerows between them to make four fields into two and two fields into one. Those were the days I first knew Thomas Mumford, when he cast his bill-hook to despair and foretold the passing of the yellow-hammer, little-owl, and dunnock from the county, said you'd never see a sparrow-hawk again within twenty miles of Cromwell's birthplace. And time proved him right.

It was in the seventies though that his work was finally finished for good, when they brought in the tractor-driven flail that made pole-traps and halberds of hedgerows. But by that time Thomas Mumford was too old to learn another trade, past caring, they said. It was then that he'd taken to retirement, like a dog to a boneless kennel, and though he must have got something from social security, I don't think it ever amounted to much. His only bit of luck was the rent on his cottage, since like most agricultural rents, it had been a fixed agreement made when he'd moved there in the nineteen fifties, and he had Handley junior to thank for being true to his father's word. He kept the cottage neat and the garden stocked, but as soon as seven o'clock came along he was down to the Green Man for his three halves of brown ale and to quote his lines of Abraham Lincoln to the world.

That Sunday evening before the elections though, sticks in my mind like a lost fortune. It was early April, and the ponies in the paddock hadn't stopped whinnying all day because of the strong Southwester gusting round the back of the stables as if it was thirsting for something. The chimney wasn't drawing properly either, I hadn't been able to get the fire to catch all afternoon, and I wasn't of a mind to sit at home alone.

In the Green Man that night, besides Jeffery the land-lord, there was only Jack Handley the Farm, built like a Clydesdale, and old Tom Mumford who had perched him-self rook-wise on a stool by the fire. It turned out he'd had a bad bit of news, as Jeffery explained, standing my Guinness aside to let it settle, hand resting on the pumps like he was shunting a steam-train, face like an engine-driver. Perhaps I might know of some way out for poor old Tom? Asked me if I knew about old violins. Or of any good antique dealers.

"Not really," I replied. "Tom been on the fiddle or something? Why d'you ask?"

"Tom wants to put an old violin up for sale, wonders how much it would fetch. Reckons it might make a bob or two." On the seat beside Tom was a bundle of sack-cloth, tied up with baler-twine, roasting from the heat of the fire.

"Been keeping this back for a rainy day," Tom explained as he took the parcel into his lap and began to tug at the ends of nylon string. "And it looks like the April showers are on us. It's either this or my medals and if an old war veteran has to sell his medals just for the council to keep in favour with the bank, then I don't know why I bothered to earn them. Time to sell the violin."

"Didn't know you once played the fiddle, Tom," I remarked.

"Didn't. Just had it lying around at home," he said as he unwrapped the instrument as if it was bundle of money that would be blown from his fingers with the first gust of the wind, then handed it to me, his eyes searching for approval as I turned it over in my hands, running my thumb over the scroll. Though no musician myself, it looked to be in fairly rough nick. The bridge was missing for a start, there were only two of the four gut strings remaining and the fingerboard was loose. I turned it over to examine the back and though it looked that maybe once this had been a fine instrument, I couldn't see it fetching very much, but Tom had obviously pinned his hopes on it and I thought he might have taken it badly if I told him what I thought.

I needn't have been so reticent. Jack Handley, never one to call a trowel a spade, began to pontificate. "Tom reckons it's worth a fair mint. Enough to keep him warm in his last years. But I reckon you don't need to be a Paganini to tell that violin's three sharps flat of a major." I was inclined to agree, though in less abrupt terms. I said I'd ask around, see what could be done about it.

It was then that the story all came out.

Apparently, old Tom had never paid a penny of his Council Tax and even though, as a pensioner, his bill had been no more than a few pounds a month, over three years or so it had all added up. Now Tom had got a letter from the council saying that in total he owed them a hundred and forty nine pounds and by court order, agreed *in absentia*, Thomas Mumford Esq. was required to pay fifty pounds a month for the next three months. He fished the letter from his pocket and asked me to read it through. The letter went on to inform that a bailiff would be calling that week to collect the agreed sum and was empowered, if the moneys were not to hand, to take away any item of suitable value.

To my accountant's mind, it struck me as odd that it had been settled in court '*in absentia*' of the debtor. Seemed like a rushed up job. I suggested to old Tom that he might not need to pay it all at once and when the bailiff turned up it would be enough to say he wanted to appeal against the court decision, get the figure readjusted. Tom just shrugged his shoulders. It seemed as if he was bent on selling the old violin.

"You work in London," Jack Handley suggested, "why don't you drop it into Sotheby's for Tom. Get the experts to have a look at it."

Bond Street is not far away from my office in Piccadilly, and it struck me as a good idea. What did Tom think of it?

He sat hunched and troubled. It wasn't that he didn't trust me he said. Only that, he would like to come along too.

It was on the way down to London that Tom told me how he'd acquired the old fiddle and it came out like a story he'd been wanting to recount for thirty years but never had the guts to tell.

Apparently, a young rifle-man, already grown old from the horrors he'd seen in the desert in North Africa, lance-corporal Thomas Mumford had been among the Special Force that landed in Naples in 'forty-four. Stayed there till the end of the war in the occupying forces and it was only when they came to leave the city that the Colonel had given lance-corporal Mumford a special mission. Some old Neapolitan noblewoman, a Bourbon by all accounts, who'd lost all her family in the war, had begged the Colonel to take a parcel back to England and see it was delivered to her only surviving relative. The Colonel, not really of a mind to go out of his way, had been at a loss to know what to do with the small wooden chest. Then he found out that lance-corporal Mumford was by chance acquainted with the Italian nephew and he entrusted it into his hands. Back in Blighty, box for young Antonio in tow, lance-corporal Mumford sets off to find the ice-cream seller in Brampton he'd known as a youth. Found out he'd been killed in a motorbike accident weeks before the war and not knowing what else to do, ignorant of both the whereabouts of his former Colonel and the address of the Neapolitan noble-woman, he'd put the box away in the compartment beneath the stairs and let it pass from mind. Thought someone would call for it. Then twenty years later, he wondered what the stink was coming from the cupboard. Seemed to be coming from the box. He prized off the lid and chucked out the mouldy jars of pickled mushrooms, the festering sun-dried tomatoes, and the suppurating lumps of salami. Found the violin tucked away beneath, a letter for Antonio placed between its strings. Couldn't read the letter, all in Italian. Felt sorry for the fiddle getting cold beneath the stairs, wrapped it up in sackcloth and put it back to bed. Near on forgot about it all those years, over half a century it had been in Tom's care. Reckoned it must have been his by now.

It was lunch-time when we walked into the instrument department at Sotheby's and Tom placed the sack-cloth bundle on the counter asking if they'd like to have a look at it, said he thought it might be worth something.

The bespectacled expert, pinafore smocked and ruddy cheeked, horrified by the bailer-twine and sack-cloth keeping the rain from the varnish of the old violin held it in his hands, flipped it over like an omelette in a pan, and grunted something about it having been a nice instrument once. Then said he'd have to take it into the store room and ask his superior. Two minutes later he trotted out again and told us they wouldn't be keeping us waiting for long, the other fellow was having a look at it, and meanwhile he opened up, became a bit more talkative, asked Tom where he'd picked it up. Tom got nervous, but he spat out the story exactly as he'd told me in the car on the way down. Then cadenced his monologue:

"I 'spect after fifty years and no one's come a knocking on my door , the violin's mine."

"You're almost certainly right," the bespectacled expert assured him and went off to consult with his colleague.

It was hardly a month later we buried Tom. There were only a handful of us at his graveside and as they lowered the coffin into the hole I fought to hold back the tears. If I had never taken Tom to Sotheby's perhaps we wouldn't have been burying him, I thought. It had happened like this.

The bespectacled expert had returned twenty minutes later and had sat Tom down, said they'd found a record for the violin in the catalogues, explained each violin had a label inside and each label had a number. Turned out that the last record of that particular violin had indeed been a noble Bourbon family in Naples with a note to say the instrument was thought to have been lost with the family in the allied raids of forty-four. Seemed to add up with Tom's story and the instrument a real Guarneri. Said the last one to have come up for auction had been in New York three years before, fetched over two million dollars.

It took a bit of time to sink in. Tom took the root of horse-radish from his pocket and bit into it. Tears were forming in his eyes. Said, what the hell's he going to do now with two million dollars. Wouldn't buy another life now. Reached in the pocket of his jacket for the medals he'd bought along too, in case the violin hadn't been enough to pay his tax. Showed them to the bespectacled expert, said, you reckon these would pay the Council Tax bill?

I'm sure it was then Thomas Mumford decided to die. I noticed the white's of his eyes turn grey and could tell he was remembering his American Dream. Saw Beverly Summers across the Atlantic calling her sweetheart Tom, saying now he had enough to pay his passage. Always did said Tom. In the box beneath the stairs.

And in the Green Man later that evening Tom sat pale as ermine, mumbling Beverly Summers' name like a mantra. No more the words of great statesmen and poets. Began to rock back and forth in his chair. Beverly, Beverly, he repeated to himself. Said he'd be crossing the water soon.

Thatcher's Trust

As he reminds the locals in the pub, Benjamin Arnold, still facing the bowling on seventy five not out, can reckon most of his innings has been scored on a pitch of forty-five degrees to the vertical. He's carried his bat through long-straw and Norfolk reed and has thatched up a good score of Huntingdonshire roofs. It was the same year as Leslie Ames was keeping wicket for England he opened his innings and he isn't going to have the umpire lift a finger at him yet. Likes a long hop as his lunchtime tipple, and was sorry when the Paine's brewery got bowled out. Says the only bails ever dislodged from his stumps were hay-bales and he can weave a fine wicket with hazel. It isn't time yet to draw stumps on Benjamin Arnold.

Such is the talk between old Benjamin Arnold and the locals, looked on by Arnold's nephew Daniel who has brought his uncle for a day out to watch the cricket in the village. With the play stopped for lunch, Arnold and nephew Daniel have adjourned to the Montague Arms, but with the local team on ninety-three for seven there's little to cheer about. The consensus in the pub is the Pakistani under twenty-ones are too much of a match for the village side.

It's while they are gathered round the bar discussing cricket that Geoff Hammond recognises the old thatcher who once did so much work in the village. He crosses the darts floor to greet him.

"Well my! It's you isn't it, Benjamin?"

"I remember you. You were the young scamp used to take away the ladders while I was on the roof."

"You wanna go and have a look at old Ma Stapleton's. They're thatching it up at the moment."

"Who's doing that then?"

"Couldn't tell you, to be honest. A group of lads from out Northamptonshire, they tell me."

Old Benjamin Arnold, retired ten years now, remembers the half-hipped roof of Rookery House and the three times in his life he thatched it. He can't divorce recollections of the house from the fond memories of Colonel Leonard Stapleton and lovely wife Dorothy and is suddenly consumed by a reverie of the past. Seeing the cricket already lost to the visitors, and preferring not to watch the indignity of the village's bowling being hit for six, he decides to pay a homage to Rookery House. Tells nephew Daniel, he'll rejoin him at the cricket a little later, then swigs at the last of his beer, gives fond regards to Mrs. Hammond and takes his walking stick from the umbrella rack.

It's a half a mile walk to Rookery House from the Montague Arms and it's a scorching August day, but Benjamin Arnold is determined on his mission. He presses his hat to the crown of his balding head and takes the footpath down towards the river.

Mulling through his mind are the memories of the three times he thatched Rookery House.

It's July 1938. Young Benjamin Arnold, only seventeen, is working his first full summer with his father. They cycle through the water-meadows at Hemingford, making a bee-line for Houghton Mill. Across the mill-race and a quarter of a mile down Fortune's Lane and opposite the old forge, they come to Rookery House amongst a shade of elms. It's just been bought by a couple new to the village, Colonel Leonard Stapleton and young bride Dorothy. The Colonel wants to have his new house re-thatched. He is strong on riding and fox-hunting and has spent time serving in India. He's also strict on discipline and wants to see the house thatched properly. Standing on the lawn dressed in smart flannels and a bowler hat, the Colonel waves his shooting stick in the direction of the dormer window and instructs Wally Arnold on exactly how he'd like to see it thatched. He doesn't want the valley leaking water or the sparrows making nests from precious straw. After all, he wants to raise a family and a good strong house is the place to start. It's got to last a long time because he's not going moving around the country and plans to make Houghton his base. Says he wants the best Huntsman or Widgeon straw and the thatcher isn't to skimp on spars or pegs. Warns the thatcher he's a stickler for detail. What's more, he wants the roof taking down to its timbers and Arnold should replace any rafters, ridge-boards or purlins he thinks need attention.

It's during this briefing, Dorothy comes out from the kitchen with three glasses of home-made lemonade on a tray, demurely offers them round, then stands to one side, head bowed, tray held over her chest as she waits for the workmen to finish their squash. She's nineteen years old and has been married four months. She stares squarely at the ground but when she holds out the tray to collect the empty glasses young Benjamin, all dark skin and biceps, thinks he sees a whimper of a smile. Benjamin knows these middle class girls. They lack the experience of the rough and tumble, but are as game as any other chicken for a roll in the hay. Hopes the Colonel might soon be sent to war and his wife be left on Home Guard for the season.

But he's soon disappointed. The Colonel is on leave for the summer and with nothing much better to do, he stands at the bottom of the ladder directing operations. He's as regimental with his workmen as he is with his wife and makes his thatchers run around like infantrymen. Refuses to grant them the leanest moment's rest, even after backbreaking labours. He expects them on duty at nine in the morning and sends them off watch at six. He gives them an hour to eat their sandwiches at lunchtime and at eleven o'clock and three-thirty precisely he whistles to young wife Dorothy to bring a glass of lemonade for each of them. During these breaks, while young Benjamin does little to conceal his interest in the soldier's wife, the Colonel treats them to a single anecdote from his time in India, the conclusion of which is the signal for Dorothy to collect up her glasses and for the thatchers to get back to work.

It's only the second week of work, the timbers newly renovated and the straw recently delivered, that Wally Arnold has a disagreement with the Colonel. There's four tons of Widgeon lying in the yard waiting to be yelmed up and the Colonel tells Arnold he's run out of straw for his horses and is going to help himself to a barrow-load or two. Despite the thatcher's protests that it will all have to go on too thin if the Colonel is of such an attitude, Stapleton carts away half a ton of straw. Then, in that cantankerous way of his, insists Wally Arnold doesn't compromise the roof.

Meanwhile, Benjamin Arnold, biceps bursting from his white poplin shirt, red neckerchief tied round his throat, a flag of invitation to young Mrs. Stapleton, spends the summer trying to impress. But father Wally has understood his son's desire and doesn't want threats of martial violence from the Colonel just because of Ben. He finds plenty for his son to do and keeps him posted to the far end of the paddock to get on with the spar-making and when the spar-making and yelming-ups all finished, if there's a moment when the Colonel is not at his usual vigil, Wally sends his son on errands to the village with shopping lists of tobacco, chocolate or newspapers.

Then, after five weeks of work and with little more roof to cover, Wally Arnold runs out of straw half way along the back. He blames it on the Colonel for having carted off half a ton for his horses and the Colonel blames it on the thatcher for being improvident. A nasty argument threatens to flare up, but eventually the Colonel backs down and offers to take the thatcher to collect some more.

They say nothing to Benjamin and leave him in the paddock to get on with his spar-making.

He's been sitting there a while, whittling on his hazel, when a shadow falls over his work. He looks up and sees Dorothy has brought him a glass of lemonade. He's worked up a thirst in the afternoon sun and Dorothy picks up a finished spar, holds it in her delicate flower-like hands.

"So this is what you're making? Will you show me how you make them?"

Benjamin demonstrates how he splits the length of hazel, first in half, then each half into thirds, so each spar is triangular in cross section. Then laying a spar across his lap, with three brisk strokes of a sickle-shaped knife, he whittles each end to a point. Then he lays the knife aside, holds the spar in both hands like it is a bicycle about to be ridden and twists his hands in opposite directions to bend the spar double. He shows her how a flat hand fits in the crook of the peg, just enough to bite the straw. Says there's nothing better for holding the straw to the roof, now would she herself like to have a go?

Demurely, Dorothy smiles a kind of refusal, explains Wally and the Colonel have gone over to Leicestershire to pick up some straw. Says she'd like to take her thatcher to bed, but fears the straw in his hair would litter the pillow, then holds out her hand and drags the thatcher through the hedge of elm suckers to the uncut corn-field beyond. Knows she shouldn't be doing any of this, knows she'll go to Hell if the vicar finds out, but is of a mind not to care. They lie down in a hare run and when Dorothy feels the rough thatcher's hand against the softness of her breast she knows she won't remain faithful to her husband for long. For the rest of the afternoon, hidden by the corn, they conjure acts of biblical antiquity that will later cause the homebound Benjamin to trail behind his father and Wally Arnold to wonder at the dearth of finished spars, the fidelity of the Colonel's young wife.

Nothing's ever mentioned, but after that day, something changes in the Colonel's manner. He becomes harsh and brusque and at break-times no longer treats them to an anecdote, just stares moodily into the lawn. He hovers around the thatchers more anxiously, pestishly than before, and is forever finding fault with the work. Dorothy remains indoors now, apparently suffering from hayfever. There's no more lemonade either.

Benjamin doubts he'll ever see Dorothy again. The work drags on and at last they arrive at the thankful day when the thatching gets finished and Wally and Benjamin load the last of their tools on their bike-trailer. To their surprise the Colonel appears on the lawn with a silver tray laden with a bottle of sherry and three glasses. In better mood now; seeing the exquisite finish of his roof and the back of Dorothy's suitor, he declares a topping-out ceremony. He pours them each a schooner of sherry and proposes a toast to the roof.

"To the King and to our fine thatcher Arnold!"

He doesn't mention Benjamin but hands Arnold senior the last instalment of his payment. The thatcher's guzzle down the sherry and say they've enjoyed working for the Colonel, that the roof's turned out well and it shouldn't give him problems with leaks. The Colonel doesn't offer a top-up of sherry and the thatchers are too reticent to ask but at that moment, Dorothy comes outside to collect the empty glasses and curtsy before the two thatchers who have made such a nice roof for their new house. She doesn't dare risk a smile at Benjamin but tidies away the glasses and turns inside. The Colonel shakes hands with the two Mr. Arnolds, thanks them for such a fine job and wishes them a nice weekend. The two thatchers climb on their bikes and set off pedalling down Fortune's lane, Benjamin trying to read his father's thoughts.

It is twenty years later, we're on doorstep of the sixties and with his father now retired, Benjamin Arnold has been working on his own for the last fifteen years.

He's working on a house in Hemingford one late Autumn evening when a new Ford Anglia draws up by the kerb. The Colonel steps out, lights himself a cigarette and calls out to Benjamin working on the ladder, beckons him down with a wave of his hand. Benjamin wonders what he wants, then climbs down the ladder, shakes the Colonel's hand and the retired soldier offers him a ciggy. Stapleton congratulates the thatcher on how well his roof's held up for the last two decades but has the idea it could do with ridging and wiring. Asks how much work Benjamin's got himself lined up in the next few months.

The Colonel is a man of darker character than he was in the days of Arnold's youth. More severe, and more foreboding, as if the war made him draw into himself, or maybe, as Arnold is later to find out, as if he has an inkling of the illness that will one day kill him. But if he knows about his fate now, he bears it calmly, as if it is something inevitable he has long since been resigned to. It is also possible that the Colonel is entirely unaware of its clawing existence. Though, as Arnold is to reflect when he later hears the news of the Colonel's death, that windswept day in late autumn, as they stood outside the house in Hemingford sharing a cigarette and a few words of business, the cancer must already have been growing in his lung.

It is March when Arnold starts work on Rookery House. The Colonel has given up his horses and now spends all day sitting indoors doing crosswords or in the greenhouse attending to his collection of cacti. He comes to inspect the work's progress only occasionally and his compliments are veiled in silence, expressed as a nod or a wave of his hand. His anecdotes too have gone forgotten and the strict hours of duty have been relaxed. Arnold is free to go and come as he wishes. There are three teenage children all back from boarding school on account of the Easter holidays and Dorothy is consigned indoors all day supervising piano practice, cookery and needlework. Arnold glimpses her only rarely, a wave through the kitchen window perhaps as he punishes a shoulder of straw up the ladder. Or a smile as she collects in the washing. It's sixteen year-old, eldest daughter Irene who now brings out the thatcher's elevenses - since the purchase of an electric kettle, a cup of tea now instead of home-made lemonade.

Dorothy hasn't aged and motherhood has slimmed her, given her a grace she never had in the early days of her marriage and there is a contentment about her face. She looks tired, but Arnold puts it down to school holidays, the constant supervision of teenage children. He never catches sight of that coquettish flight which took hold of him twenty years earlier. As if motherhood or the war has taken away from her all those pleasures. Or perhaps, because she knows it's impossible, with the children and her husband around.

But still, Arnold longs for a repeat of that afternoon twenty years before and wishes the children and the Colonel would have reason to go rambling one afternoon. It never happens, and each day, as he gets back into his Morris Minor van to return home, Arnold hopes the next day might bring a change of luck. He ponders the war. With the Colonel fighting in North Africa, and the battalions of American GIs who were stationed in the region. Wonders if he's not the only man to have cuckolded the Colonel.

The work too is different this time. The ridging and wiring takes only three weeks as opposed to the eight it took him and his father to thatch the whole roof twenty years before. The valleys either side of the dormer windows need a little patching and the ridge needs doing. But it's easy working over his own work. He sticks to the same pattern on the ridge, combs down the thatch and patches up a small hole in the eave of the porch where the sparrows have been pulling out the straws to make their nests. He can still recall precisely the problems they encountered when they did the roof before and remembers how they went about solving them. He has his father's words in his ears as he works, that same slow advice from which he learnt so much and as he quietly dissects the ridge, he sees how it has resisted the weather so well for so long. Knows the work was done by a master and understands why the Colonel wanted an Arnold back to thatch.

When the work is finished, the Colonel invites him to a glass of sherry. It happens to be raining that afternoon and Arnold is invited inside the Colonel's study. He is given a seat before the fire burning in the inglenook fireplace and Stapleton pours only a single glass - which he explains by saying he himself has given up strong drink. The ceremony is not expected to last long. The two men sit opposite each other and Arnold tells an anecdote about a farmer he once knew in the village. The Colonel is hardly listening and Benjamin cuts short his monody. They shake hands cordially and the Colonel puts a handsome sum of money in Arnold's pocket, but as Arnold climbs into his van, it's with regret that he's leaving the job without another souvenir memory of Dorothy.

He is not to know though he will never see the Colonel again: that in two years time the man will be dead, that he will pre-decease his wife by over thirty years, and it will be another twenty before he sets eyes on Dorothy again.

It is a dark May morning, 1980, when Benjamin Arnold gets a phone-call from a woman with a bright tinctured voice asking if she has the right number for a Mr. Arnold and wondering if he remembers her husband.

It's September when Arnold, not many years off retirement himself begins work on Rookery House for the third time in his life. It's a big job this time. It's over forty years since it was completely re-thatched and in the last five years it's begun to let in rain. But Arnold has a lad to work for him now. His own strength is beginning to fail him and he can't carry so much up a ladder in a day as once he did.

They arrive on the first morning in Arnold's Bedford van with a trailer-load of straw and a roof-rack of hazel. Mrs. Stapleton says they'll need some refreshment before they start unloading all that and shows them into her kitchen. She serves them mugs of Continental coffee with rich tea biscuits and doesn't stop talking all morning.

The Colonel died of cancer twenty years before and Mrs. Stapleton left a widow at forty-one. Her three children have grown up and left: one is a computer programmer in the States, another an air-hostess living near Heathrow and the other a translator in France. She sees them only irregularly and not always at Christmas. It's a lonely life she ekes out for herself in the village, making do with nothing more than her husband's military pension. But if she suffers, she does so only inwardly. She paces her days with a slow regularity and still drives the VW Beetle that she will keep until her death. Fears nothing more than burglars. With the Colonel's ghost well dead and buried, Dorothy has become more garrulous. She speaks often of her children and Arnold can see that she misses them.

It's the afternoon by the time the trailer gets unloaded, the following day before any real work gets done.

Robin, his apprentice, is sat in the paddock cutting spars, while Benjamin Arnold puts a ladder to the roof to begin removing the old wire. Dorothy is hovering around in the yard and from the bottom of the ladder Arnold winks at her. Asks if she's going to take advantage of the spar-maker in the way she did forty years before. Or are her tastes more matured? Dorothy smiles back, a sign she understands. Says, how could she now? She is far too old for such a thing. Besides, she'd like Arnold to know she never again cheated on her husband. He was a good man and if young Benjamin himself had not been so irresistible, she would have thought more than twice about having him. Dorothy is still pretty. Not as blithe as she was twenty years before. Her husband's death and maybe her children's absence has taken some of the stuffing out of her, but she still has beautiful bones and still dresses with that same gentle country elegance that attracted Benjamin Arnold as a teenager. Benjamin smiles back and begins to paw his way up the ladder.

That Autumn passes slowly. He keeps her amused with her stories and they share talk of how the village has changed in the intervening years but Mrs. Stapleton goes out more often these days. She goes shopping to the nearby villages or else to a whist drive or coffee morning. She always has her nose in something and Arnold can't help wondering if she expected her life to turn out like this. Maybe forty years before she had a different set of expectations. He wonders if she's happy.

The thatching too is nostalgic. He's now working over his own ridge of twenty years before, and his father's work of twenty before that. He sees how the pegs he sat sharpening at the bottom of the paddock as a boy have held. Few of them have fallen from place.

Arnold has always asked the question 'why?' when confronted with old work. Sees how the thatcher before him knocked the pegs in downwards and the water got into the straw. Or how another thatcher made his pegs too short and they haven't held. If only he could instil this lesson into

Robin's head. Robin's a strong enough lad, but tackles problems with his balls instead of his brains. He may or may not yet make a thatcher, Arnold thinks. Can carry more than a ton of straw up a ladder in a day, but sometimes, if he isn't watched on the roof, will lay it on so crookedly it's hardly worth the effort for all the time Arnold spends working behind him trying to straighten out the gaps and keep the line.

The thatchers work hard and in little over eight weeks the roof gets finished. Dorothy is overjoyed. She sees Rookery House restored to the glory of the first years of her marriage. She fetches a bottle of port from the cellar and insists they celebrate the work's completion. In Mrs. Stapleton's kitchen they sit round the range drinking down the port like teenagers, giggling at the stories they tell. Arnold's three-parts-gone as he climbs in his Bedford van later that evening and wonders if he'll get home without surrendering his licence to the law. But before he turns the keys, he looks in the widow's eyes and knows he won't be back in twenty years time to thatch the roof, knows the thatch could well outlast them both.

"You'll drop by when you're next in the village, won't you?" Dorothy pleads.

Arnold never does. Then one day he hears she'd been taken ill with flu. It turns to pneumonia and puts her on her death-bed. That's five years ago now.

Benjamin Arnold nears the end of Fortune's Lane, and sees Rookery House now crowded by a recent development of mock-Tudor houses. Thinks it a shame that the grove of elms is gone and has given way to this clump of ugly buildings. He shuffles along the pavement, in his mind turning over the weight of straw on the roof. He knows the roof of Rookery House by heart, could thatch it in his sleep. Can still remember the measurements, the amount of straw and pegs it took. The hours it took to get inside the valleys of the dormer windows.

But as he draws near now, he sees how the roof seems twisted out of shape. The thatchers have finished the front and are three-quarters of a way along the back. If Geoff Hammond says they've been working on it for only a couple of weeks, he is amazed. Remembers how it took him and Robin the best part of nine weeks to finish the house. But as he gets nearer he understands the reason. There are four of them working on the job. All youngish lads, with the oldest no older than forty and one who looks in his teens. Is immediately suspicious the moment he sees the side of their brand new Renault van: W.R. Mason - Tilers, slaters and thatchers. Know at once they are only odd job builders with a rudimentary knowledge of rafters, eave boards and gable ends. Doubtless know nothing more about thatching than Welsh slate and pan-tiles. Feels an immediate rush of blood to his head.

As Arnold draws nearer, he crosses the road and leans against a gate post of the old forge. Takes a packet of Rothman's from his pocket and quietly lights one up to stem his rising anger. Sees they are making a right pig's ear of it all. Wants to go and tell them what a great cock-up their work is. Worth nothing to the people who paid for it. But knows they wouldn't care a damn because as sure as eggs it won't be them who are returning in twenty years to re-thatch it. As likely as not it will be some poor bastard coming round in five years time to try and find all the leaks that have sprung from their shoddy work. But there will be nothing he can do, and it will be in vain he will try to explain to the hapless owners that their money would be better invested if they took it all off and started again from scratch.

Arnold's eyes fill with tears as he sees how they have too much straw on the eaves, too little on the ridge, have made the whole roof pitch less and knows it won't shed water like it ought. Furthermore, he can see they've got the valleys of the dormer windows all wrong. There's no way the water's going to drain down those and within a single winter they'll have moss growing from them, which will hold the moisture all through the year. Sees too how they've got the eave uneven and it curls crookedly from one end to the other like a tilde. Watches how the four of them work. The eldest, and no doubt, W.R. Mason himself is a large fat man who needs two ladders placed side by side to take his weight. Looks straight off a building site, built up like an office block from years of fish and chip abuse. Sees how he carries a loose, baggy yelm up the ladder and hammers it into the rafter using metal spikes. Knows that the rafters can't take such a hammering of metal spikes, that doubtless as not, he's splitting them all to pieces and before five years are out the roof timbers will collapse in on themselves. Sees how there are two others working on the back of the house who look like two rappers on the loose from the local borstal.

The youngest, despite the height of the summer is as pale as acid and looks as if he'd been kept shut indoors all year.

As Arnold stands to watch one of the rappers crosses the road for a fag-break. Has seen Arnold standing there and thinks he must be admiring the work. Comes to have a word with him.

"Fuckin' 'ot on that roof."

"I bet it is, with all that running around you're doing."

"You live in the village?"

"No."

Arnold is as short on words as he is for admiration for their work. Then shores himself up for a question.

"What's that straw you're putting on?"

"Long straw, mate."

"Where do you get that from then?"

"Bloke out Rushden way."

"You're putting it on too thick at the eaves, to my mind."

"Nah mate. You don't know about thatchin'. That's the way it goes. Traditional like."

Arnold resists letting on, thinks he'll play the game along further.

"How long you lads been doing this then?"

"Me an' Eric, 'bout six monfs. Will up there's been in it five years. Used to only do tiling and slating, but there's more money in thatchin'."

"Bet there is the way you guys throw it on."

"Fuckin' art though, innit?"

"'Ard? I guess so."

"No' many guys know 'ow to thatch these days. Dyin' art, innit?"

Arnold invites himself round the back to inspect the work, says he'd be interested to see how they do it. Wanders round the back of the house with new friend Rapper, who, for what he lacks in thatching skills, at least makes up for in friendliness. His eyes fill with tears when he sees what a shoddy job they are making. Wishes the Colonel was around to put them in their places. Check the work is going properly. Sees how, they've built an extension on the back of the house which joins the roof at right angles. Gives them two extra valleys to thatch. Sees how they are making a pig's ear of those as well.

"Is there anyone living in the house at the moment?"

"Not at the moment. Some architect in Huntingdon bought it. He's doing it up. Nice house, innit?"

"It *was* a nice house."

Arnold picks up a handful of the straw and twists it in his hands. Sees how it hasn't been threshed properly and knows that with the winter coming on, it will all be sprouting green with winter wheat. They'll have to come and kill it off with weed-killer. Then sees how the straw breaks when twisted. Reckons these cowboys must have bought up the straw as a job lot. Thrown out by some other thatcher. Then picks up a metal spike.

"You don't believe in hazel spars then?"

"Nah, mate. That's the old fashioned method. No one does that now. Gotta keep up with the times and them old hazel spars take too long to make. That's not to mention the time you spend cutting the hazel out the wood."

"Take you less time than it will to replace the rafters, when you smashed them all up with all these metal spikes you're banging in. They're only elm branches pulled green from the hedgerow."

"Nah mate. What you know about thatchin'?"

Arnold eyes Rapper squarely, wonders if he's going to let on the truth or whether he'll play the game along a little longer.

"Not much. Just odd bits of information I picked up over the years. Did a bit here and there."

Arnold's eyes glaze over. Knows he can't keep up the secret for long. Is too upset by the shoddy job he sees the thatchers doing. Wonders if all the patient hours, he, his father, Robin spent, arranging the straw on the roof have not all come to nothing. Even the skills that he spent so many years learning and perfecting, the art he strove to acquire goes unappreciated by this gang of odd job builders from Rushden. Thinks it might have been better if they'd stuck to slates and pan-tiles. Has ideas of throwing his cigarette into the pile of straw and watch the whole lot go up in flames. Sees there's no more point in talking any longer to these ignorant cowboys. What would they care anyway for all the advice he could give them. Sees he's wasting his time. Says to Rapper,

"Well, I doubt you'll be back here in twenty years time and I doubt I will either, to see the roof all caved in."

"Nah mate. Last a lifetime this thatch."

It's then Arnold can't help feeling his blood rise.

"Not the way you're putting it on it won't."

"What you mean?"

"I mean, I thatched this house three times in my life, know that roof better than you lot know your own plonkers.

Take my word, it'll need re-thatching in less than five
years."

The Rapper shrugs.

"Yeh, but what do I care?" he says with a flush of hon-
esty. "I ain't gonna still be working for these guys when the
owners find that out. I'll be long gone, mate. Another two
grand saved up an' I've got enough for a down payment on
a night-club in Ibiza. What do I care about their straw
roof?"

Arnold is wasting his time talking to these odd-job
builders, wants to find an excuse to get away.

"I only hope the builders that do the roof of your disco
in Ibiza remember to mix cement in the concrete. Otherwise you've got yourself a problem."

Arnold leans on his walking stick, he's happy to leave
the Rapper to juggle with his straw.

"You keep dreaming of Ibiza!" he says in parting as he
sets off once again down Fortune's Lane, trying to hide the
tears that have filled his eyes. The ghosts of his memories
now lie buried by a pile of stubble chucked on the roof by a
load of cowboys. Wishes Stapleton's phantom would rise
right now from the dead and cart away the straw for his
horses.

Iranian Lettuce

Trout was a lonesome child. Through no fault of his own, a result of his father's economy of thought when he bought a house in Grafham, the boy was destined to a childhood devoid of friends. With no other children in the village his age, Mike Trout lived out a condemned adolescence condemning wildlife to existence in a jam-jar. "For breeding," he used to tell his mother when he brought home the pots stuffed with dragon-flies, hawk-moths and stag-beetles and a few days later, habitually mounted their cadavers on the squares of card he would later consign to drawers labelled: "specimins - keep out!".

Trout had a death-wish for nature's smaller creatures that some considered cruel. Was possessed of a maniacal patience that disposed him to pass whole days herding colonies of ants into matchboxes. All for five minutes' joy with a magnifying-glass the next morning, as he turned nature against itself and focused the sun's rays to a smouldering pinpoint on the box's surface, delighting in the fomenting and sizzling of formic acid. School summer holidays, in Trout's lonely mind, were for stalking the hedgerows with a butterfly-net on red-alert. Later, he would make his captives breathe the wad of cotton-wool soaked in chloroform he concealed in a bottle. Assiduously added the occasional tortoiseshell, peacock, red-admiral to his extensive collection of assorted cabbage-whites which jostled for space in his bedroom with the jars of beetles, pupae, caterpillars. He nurtured ambitions of one day owning a praying-mantis and meanwhile honed his dreams with a vivarium of stick-insects. Estimated that in the five years of keeping his twiggy arthropods, they had collectively gorged neighbour Reverend Arkwright's hedge twice over and was happy to let the retired vicar ponder the reason why the privet grew better one side than the other.

Trout Senior turned a blind eye to his son's dark psychology, said it was part of growing up in the country. He made a mildly profitable living from a plant hire business, more specifically a JCB, hired out daily, with himself as driver, to dig drains, foundations, septic tanks for local builders, swimming pools for the well-off, roadside ditches for the Huntingdon District Council. Was content with his lot and nourished only one ambition for his son: that he didn't pass a lifetime getting piles, sitting in a tractor shifting levers and staring at the depth of blue clay.

Mike Trout, an authority on lepidoptera at fourteen years old, rolled his eyes round their sockets, sucked at his bulging tongue and knew he was going to get wet. He pedalled a mad dash between the traffic of the Northbound carriageway and headed for the shelter of the oak tree a hundred yards ahead. Could feel the asthma clawing at his chest and remembered he'd forgotten his inhaler. Behind him, the traffic on the Great North Road evaporated in a haze of spray as he raced for the leafless thatch of branches that would do little to stem the torrent of water already pouring from the black November sky. And the two miles home now seemed as forbidding as a cold shower after football at school. He jumped from his bike, hugged himself to the trunk and, through the drops cascading in waterfalls down the lenses of his specs, saw the world go funny.

He looked wishfully beyond the thick scrub of cotoneaster hedge beside him, to the cottage he'd always assumed abandoned. The only other habitation a rifle-shot away. Noticed smoke being forced back down the chimney, a light burning in the kitchen and conjectured he must've been wrong. He took stock of the wood piled against the trunk of the apple tree in the garden, the neatness of the flower-beds, the well-tilled soil. And saw how the lace curtains twitched.

The front door of the cottage opened and a crinkly woman in a pinny called out through the drops of rain now spearing the earth like javelins.

"You wanna come in for a cuppa tea, my dear! You'll get wet standing there!"

Trout once again hurled himself under the sheets of rain, pushed his bike through the narrow gate and left it leaning against the Flemish bond brickwork of the turn-of-the-century cottage. Then pelted for the door where the stout lady stood wiping her hands on the front of her pinny and bemoaning the afternoon's weather.

"Look at you!" she said, as Trout squeezed himself under cover and stood in the doorway dripping water onto the freshly polished lino. "You'd ought to take your parka off so as we can dry it by the Aga."

And the apple-pie scented lady helped him off with his coat as Trout set foot in the sparsely furnished kitchen. A simple table flanked by two cottage chairs faced a blazing range, and on the opposite wall, a faucet dripped into a cracked sink. There was no fridge, no oven, no evidence of the opulent 1990s whose doorstep we were just about to breach. Only a pine-dresser of old crockery stood proudly in that kitchen, a postcard of Yarmouth adorning its mantelpiece. In the far corner, silent as the furniture itself and staring amazedly at Trout, an old man was cradled in an armchair, clinging to the arms for dear life. Trout was on the point of an about turn when the man surprised him with speech.

"You goin' far?"

"Only Grafham," Trout replied.

"You better sit here an' dry yourself out while the rain blows over," Jack told him, pointing to one of two cottage chairs. "There's no use bein' out in this."

That was the first afternoon Trout met Jack and Peggy. Weathered a happy hour in their company while the storm blew over. He noted the way they fussed over the rich tea biscuits Peggy laid out on a plate, the way Jack got up to make the tea. Judged them a couple devoted to each other and wished his own mum and dad could be so affectionate.

That night, as the smell of rain smouldered in their cramped bedroom, Peggy lay awake, threatened by the uneven plaster in the ceiling, saw its cracks scowling down at her. Wondered if she'd done wrong to show charity to the boy and couldn't drive away the thought of PC Barton's visit the month before, warning them of thieves in the county, lads down from Nottingham hawking tea-towels, dishcloths, oven-gloves as recce for prospective burglaries. She turned to Jack and wrapped her big cauliflower hands round the atrophying biceps of the ex-hodge.

"Jack?"

"The Ouse'll be up tomorrow."

"There was something wrong with that boy's eyes. You think he's all there?

"Don't be daft, he were cold."

"When did you last check behind the kitchen dresser?"

"It's still there, Peggy. Go to sleep."

And he turned out the light on Peggy's ugly premonitions. Left her to dream of all the evil things that could befall one, old and alone in the country, and to imagine the mice running off with her porcelain dolls.

She awoke the next morning to find the kitchen exactly as she'd left it, the cat curled up by the fire and the world in its nest. Picking up the broom, she swept vigorously at the lino on the kitchen floor and wished all her uncharitable thoughts to be pushed beneath the doormat. She never said another word to Jack about Trout's eyes. Chastised herself sorely for assuming his astigmatism a sign of malevolence.

The following Spring saw Trout frequently strolling the farm tracks that led to Brampton Woods, scouring the hedgerows and verges for brimstones, small blues, orangetips and meadow-browns. He would often come across Jack, shunting by the horns a bicycle laden with firewood, gripping by the ears a rabbit destined for the pot or studying the imminent weather from beneath the refuge of his cap's shallow peak. The old hodge would always stop, comment on the forming cirrus, the late-blossoming hawthorn, the scent of a dog fox and Trout would nod sagely, amazed how an ex-farm labourer could know so many facts. Saw in those leaky brown eyes a lonely old man whose only solace was to wander the farm-tracks and take account of nature. Knew Jack never ventured further than the fields around his cottage, and other than the occasional wave to a passing farmhand, had precious little contact with the outside world. And knew he himself was company of sorts.

Besides, warming their backs in the April sun, Trout was happy to lay down his butterfly net and listen to Jack tell stories of the local farmland, reminiscing about the days when the work was done by cart horse. Was mesmerised by the sound of Jack's voice, its soft Huntingdonshire vowels, its consonants like butter, its rounded musical tone. Felt at ease, knowing he didn't have to answer back and chat, just nod his head and listen to the long lines of words. Felt a certain warmth for the man.

Their affection was mutual. Jack was proud the boy took an interest in nature, saw him as his protégé, an ally against the growing ranks of school-boys who couldn't tell a kestrel from a cuckoo, elder from alder, a weasel from a stoat.

It was Mrs. Squire in the post office, Ellington, though who burst the bubble of Trout's great illusion. He'd only gone to buy a jar of Horlicks but in the course of their conversation he mentioned old Jack up at Grange Farm Cottage, and Mrs. Squire suddenly went all cold. She gave him a squirmy look like Trout'd got involved with something evil, then leaned low over the counter to speak in a whisper. She put straight what had never occurred to young Trout.

Jack and Peggy were not husband and wife.

After Mrs. Squire told Trout the truth about Jack, a great cloud of unknowing began to form in the adolescent's mind. Had Jack ever done it with his sister? Or was he one of those who'd never had it? Answers in either direction made Trout all strange, understood now why Mrs. Squire went squirmy.

After that, Trout didn't go back to see Jack much more. Gave up butterflies and stick-insects and took to reading books.

Years went by, and Trout was in his last year at school. He'd turned out bright, done well in his GCSEs, and made his parents proud. Looked like he'd get to university - a Trout family first.

But one thing still burned away in Trout's pining heart. He'd never had a girl and he didn't want to end up at seventy being like Jack. He had the field to lie down in but no girl to take to the pastures. Saw how all his friends had got over that hurdle, but still couldn't straddle it himself. Identified his problem as never getting on the guest-list to the parties where 'it' happened. Reasoned it his reputation as a swot, and resolved to roughen up his image. He wondered if he ought to take up smoking, but on account of his asthma, dismissed it as unwise. And drugs were out of the question. Cannabis, round Grafham, was rarer than adolescent females.

It was a leaflet picked up from the table of an animal rights group on Huntingdon market that presented the solution - a mail-order firm in Cornwall supplying hemp seeds to order and Trout hit upon the notion that a crop of home-grown leaves and a willingness to deal would earn him an income of party invitations. Reckoned that by dishing out the dope at parties he'd surely get a wink from a girl.

The only obstacle in Trout's zany scheme was how he might propagate the seeds without his mother finding out. It was then that he remembered an out-of-the-way cottage and a senile gardener who would be only to happen to help him.

"Jack, I bought something for you," Trout said, tipping the seeds from the small tobacco tin onto the surface of the table. "It's a rare kind of Iranian lettuce. They'd do well planted out behind the potting shed. They grow five feet tall, and got big, strap-like leaves. Only, you don't just go putting'm in salad. They're more like herbs. You gotta hang the leaves up to dry. Wait for the winter. Add them to a soup. Good for keeping colds at bay."

"Alright then. Only you'd better come 'n' 'elp me when you thinks they're ready for pickin'."

"No question of that, Jack. You just make sure you give'm a good watering every morning and they'll be up ready for harvesting by July. That's what the instructions say."

Deep in Trout's scheming mind was the notion he'd creep back one night to pinch the drying herbs from Jack's potting shed and replace them with lupin leaves from his mother's garden. Knew the presbyopic Jack would never tell the difference.

Then three months later, and the day after Trout had helped Jack harvest his leaves, Peggy had her accident.

She'd been crossing the A1, pushing her bicycle, and hadn't seen the car coming up behind the lorry. She'd been taken off to intensive care in Addenbrookes, but there wasn't much hope of her coming out of the coma and Jack was beside himself. He stuck it out for two days on his own at Grange cottage, but then was up the farm asking Handley for a lift to Cambridge. In the hospital ward, Jack sat down by Peggy's bed and never moved from her side. When the nurses kindly told him visits were finished for the day, he bluntly responded he was staying with his sister. Threatened to slash his wrists if they threw him off the ward, so the ward-matron found him a room in the hospital.

It was a burning July night two days later and Trout was sat in a pub out Needingworth way with Digger, Liam and Zoë, washing vodka and cokes, pints of Guinness and tequila-slammers down their necks. Fresh from school exams, virginal and desperate, Trout was burning with a desire to conquer women and the recklessness of knowing he wasn't going to die just yet. Saw his hope in Zoë.

Fifteen years old, fantastic red curls and curves like an ampersand, Zoë was endowed with a talent for sex already familiar to most of the boys in the sixth form. Trout knew she'd not refuse an offer of a trip to the cornfields on a hot July night - if only he could lose their two chaperones. But Trout thought it all more complicated than it really was. Never realised that at the mention of a tumble in the hay Zoë would've improvised a cornfield from the back seat of his car, while Digger and Liam sat drinking in the pub. Instead, Trout saw his hope in the Persian salad drying in Jack's shed. Knew the old man was in Addenbrokes, and thought it would be simple enough to stop by and get the weed. Take it up to Brampton Wood and smoke it. Then once he'd lost Digger and Liam in a haze of dope, the cornfield would be all for him and Zoë.

"You lot fancy a smoke? I know where there's a decent bit of weed," Trout suggested. And they tumbled out of the pub, all four of them ripe for adventure.

A hand-brake turn at the car-park exit spun Trout's Fiat 127 in the direction of Grafham and the feeling of imminent catastrophe vanished in a haze of beer. He accelerated down the hill at Houghton, pushed the needle up to eighty and knew they were going to have fun. Then failed to negotiate the bend into Hartford, mounted the kerb at seventy and relinquished control of car to the intuitive genius of the beer he'd been drinking.

At Grange Farm Cottage, he pulled off the road into the entrance of the farm track that led to Brampton Woods. The moon was full, he could negotiate the track without lights, and no one would discover them smoking up there by the copse. He stopped the engine, told the others he'd only be a minute.

"Just get the weed, man."

Trout took his pocket knife out of the glove-box and, stumbling from the car, stalked towards the potting shed, where, the week before, on the afternoon before Peggy's accident, he'd helped Jack hang the weed. Heard Digger running up behind him, tripping over molehills in the grass.

"Fuck, Trout! You can't just take things out of other people's greenhouses in the middle of the night. What if they catch us!"

Trout turned, and opening his buttock, propelled a fart in the direction of the orchard. Heard an owl call back.

"They're both in hospital. What they going to do about it?"

Zoë had got out of the car to retch. The sound of gurgling vomit rent the still night air and a few yards from Digger, a foul-smelling cocktail looped in a great arc towards the rows of asparagus.

"Urrrgh!" Digger cried out and went hurtling off round the other side of the cottage where Liam was now watering the fennel with a spray of urine.

Trout pushed open the door of the potting shed and stepped inside. He ran his hand along the rafters to search for the twine securing the weed to the roof, then clipped the string with his pocket-knife and brought the bundles of weed to the worktop.

Meanwhile, Zoë, upright again and listing in the direction of the hedge, had lit a cigarette to take the taste of puke from her palate. Liam tripped and swore. Having relieved his bladder of the snakebites and vodka, he was now snooping round the cottage searching for a souvenir of rustic life. He pushed opportunely at the back door and felt the wood swing inwards. Someone had forgotten to secure the latch.

Trout collected up the bundle of home-grown and was heading back to the car when he noticed the open back-door and realised they'd invited themselves inside. A sobering panic broke over him.

"You lot, I've got the weed," he called out, breaching the threshold of the property, unaware that upstairs a sad and drunken man turned in his sleep, nightmares of adolescent voices breaking on the waves of his dreams.

"You wanna come 'n' 'ave a jar o' this mate."

Trout crept through the immaculate living room and turned into the moonlit kitchen, where he saw Liam looking for money among the drawers of the dresser.

"Hey, Liam. You can't do this. This is Jack's house. He'd be wild if he knew we'd broken in…"

"Thought you said 'e was in 'ospital?"

"He is. But…"

"Then we're alright, innit?"

"Have some o' this…" and Digger raised a glass to Trout.

He was sitting comfortably at the kitchen table where the remains of Jack's wake still littered the table - a half-empty demijohn of elderflower wine and a single tumbler. Digger had poured himself a glass of the hooch and now tipped it back in a single gulp. There was a spluttering, choking, as he wiped his chops.

"Fuck, that's strong."

Trout had the idea he'd better leave them to it. He wasn't going to leave his fingerprints on Jack's glasses. Or be searched by the police with Jack's money in his pocket. He'd take Zoë up the wood on her own and let them get on with their larceny. He turned to head back into the garden, but as he wandered through the sitting-room he found Zoë now crashed out on the sofa. Said, "Bloody idiots those two. You fancy going up the wood to have a smoke?"

Zoë pulled him down on top of her. She put her tongue in his ear, began to scour his lobes with the tip of her wand and whispered that she didn't give a damn for Eastern leaves, said she wanted his cherries instead. She grabbed hold of his trousers, began to grapple at the fly and Trout lost himself to the rush of adrenaline. Dropped his precious Farsi salad to the floor, ripped at her shirt, and tugged at her bra until it came away in his hand. The big fleshy eye of her nipple stared up at him and Trout began to suck. Zoë unbuttoned his shirt and massaged his blubbery chest with her lovely fingers while Trout let the beer do the work as he pulled off Zoë's jeans and threw them to the floor. Poked around with his grubby finger and hoped he was doing the right thing.

Zoë knew the tumble wouldn't last long and began to regret she hadn't opted for the dope. She felt for Trout's cock, found it already sticky with come but dragged it inside her and at once felt Trout's sledge-hammer pounding rocking the boat of Jack's sofa. Heard the floorboards knocking out their angry rhythm and wondered if the couch would hold.

Digger was drowning himself in the pleasure of Jack's home-brewed elderflower wine, knocking it back like it was cough mixture when Liam put his hand down the back of the kitchen dresser, felt the cold touch of gun-metal and knew exactly what it was.

"Fuck, Digger, take a look at this," he whispered as he brought the .303 Lee-Enfield out into the moonlight to aim it through the window at the crazy stars.

"Shit, man, how d'you know it ain't loaded?" Digger felt the blood in his veins cool a few degrees. "Don't you know all farmers keep a loaded gun in the kitchen!"

Liam grinned then put the rifle back down behind the dresser. Digger sank another glass of hooch as Liam left the kitchen and began to climb the stairs to look for jewellery.

Trout was just pulling up his trousers round the dampness of his loins when he heard Liam scream and roll down the stairs like thunder.

"Fuck man, there's someone up there!"

Trout wrestled with the buckle of his belt and laughed out loud, certain that Liam had just been fooled by Jack's cat Tansy. Walked to the bottom of the stairs where he met Liam's stare, white with fear.

"Let's get outta here!" he heard Digger slur through the darkness.

"You just set eyes on Tansy!" And began to mount the stairs. Never took accord of the heavy length of metal, Liam had just thrust in his hand. He'd never been upstairs in Jack's house before.

At the top of the stairs, he swaggered into the first bedroom, saw Jack sitting up in bed, frozen with terror.

"Who are you?" Jack's voice tremored.

"Jack, what the fuck are you doing here?" Trout hollowed, suddenly becoming aware of the rifle in his hands.

"My God, that's you Trout."

"You're supposed to be in Addenbrokes!"

"What are you doing in here?"

"Just came to see you're alright."

"You wait, I'll tell the police it was you."

Trout went cold. If police got involved, things would get heavy. What with the weed and all that. And how would his parents take it? Suddenly felt the gun take aim at the head of the raging geriatric.

"Peggy died today. Don't you understand boy?"

"Jack, you make a promise you aren't going to tell the police, and I won't pull the trigger."

"Trout, that gun's loaded. You pull the trigger and I'm dead.

"Make a promise..."

"I told you, Peggy died today..."

"I said make a promise..."

"Peggy...!"

"... a promise!"

Jack made a lurch for the gun. Trout went nervous, backed against the wall, knocked a vase from the dresser and saw the chrysanthemums spill to the floor. Jack was out of bed now and had hold of a chair which he was raising above his shoulder like he wanted to bring it crashing down on Trout's head. But Trout was backed into a corner, couldn't see how he was going to escape. He pulled the trigger, saw Jack's face explode in front of his head. Heard Zoë scream downstairs. Digger and Liam rushing up behind him. Saw the whole horror of what he'd done.

"Fuck, let's get out of here, quick." Liam was already shoving Trout down the stairs. Urging him away, telling Zoë they had to get in the car quick, pushing Digger towards the back door.

They never saw Digger searching in his pockets for a box of matches, calmly and coldly, putting a light to the cover of the sofa before hurrying outside to the potting

shed where he'd noticed the tin of lawn-mower petrol. Zoë
and Liam bundling themselves into the back of the Fiat
urging Trout they had to get away, shouting, "where the
fuck's Digger?!"

As he started the car, Trout could see the light a quarter
of a mile away in Grange Farm and knew they'd heard the
shot. Thought he could see Handley charging across the
field in the moonlight, then was blinded by the glare and an
enormous explosion. Digger, having hurled the tin of petrol
through the window of the cottage was now pushing himself through the tiny door of the Fiat saying, "move it
Trout!"

Trout spun the wheels, whipped the car round onto the
farm track and in his rear-view mirror watched the awful
pyre of his maniacal madness fade to a dot.

Trout never did get caught. Never even had a visit from the
police. No one had seen them and there was no other reason to suspect them. The Law had been of the same opinion as the locals. It must have been those lads down from
Nottingham, surprised in the middle of the robbery who
had shot Jack dead and torched the house. But no one, not
even in the Midlands ever went to court over it.

There was an irony in what unfolded later. After the cottage
burnt down, and the police inspectors had crawled all over
it and the insurance assessors had had their say, the Church

Commission decided to demolish it. Trout Senior got the job.

Trout Senior had never known Jack. Neither had he ever known of his and Trout Junior's one time mutual affection.

It was a wintry morning with a hoar frost gripping the ground. Trout parked his JCB by the oak tree and took one last stroll round the charred and burnt timbers. Poked his nose in the still-standing potting shed. Saw Jack's old tools still hanging in the racks and on the shelves, the stacks of flower-pots, the bags of seeds. There, open on the shelf was the pen-knife he'd had as a boy, engraved with his own initials, and which he once gave to Trout junior as a present. Trout Senior was too frightened to draw the obvious explanation that stared him in the face. He preferred to live without knowing the truth and was happy to let time convince him that Trout junior had dropped the pocket-knife while out collecting butterflies.

And Jack, in the magpie ways of country people, had found it.

The history of Wisbech according to Alf Crack

Alf Crack was a man who could talk. Entertained everyone he came across with his chronicles of quotidian Wisbech. He told yarns as if they sprung from his stomach, his great whale belly belching stories, and parcelled in his rough fenland talk, the history of the town unfolded like a vast Icelandic saga. "He could talk the donkey off its hind leg," the local folk said of him, and it wasn't so far from the truth.

Crack lived out Grunty Fen way, in one of those thirties-style council semis on the edge of town that looked like poor apologies for houses. Fat as a Michelin Man, he'd been alone there fifteen years, ever since his wife became possessed by the notion of a happier life elsewhere, and walked out on him for a coalman in Chatteris, carrying their two nappy-wrapped daughters and an empty post-office book for baggage. She left behind the seventeen-stone of pork fat and Guinness of a husband to chin-wag his way through the left debts and years of unpaid bills.

Crack had barely done a full day's work since, used his time to cultivate aversions to repaying his creditors and made it his vocation to outwit them. Considered solvency a chore. He had a conscience as bare as his pate and a philosophy as expansive as his girth. "When you're in debt, what's the use in working? You're only filling someone else's pocket," was the motto Alf Crack lived by. And true to his word, there were few could remember the last time Crack came home, masonry dust in his sparse hair, gloss-stained overalls, silicon coated and smelling of work. Nowadays, when referred to Alf Crack, 'builder' was more epithet than honest job-description and only now and then, when the fancy took him, did he fill his time with knocking out a fireplace, plaster-boarding a new partition wall, rendering a garage, erecting a conservatory or larch-lap fence. Boasted he did a good job of highway planning - especially bypasses. 'Bypassing the planning department at Town Hall, Huntingdon,' he'd add with a grin the size of a bucket handle.

It was one of those June mornings when the sun gets up before dawn and Crack, about to make the morning brew, was searching the sink of dirty dishes that constituted the extent of his kitchen, for any mug-like receptacle with less than an inch of mould. A few minutes later, kettle on the boil, and tea-bag stuffed inside dolly-bird Yarmouth souvenir, Crack was looking out through the panes of his kitchen window, line of vision broken by his surname.

He gazed over the lifeless carapaces of defunct Ford Capris lining the kerbside, and pondered the archetypal nature of the cul-de-sac's landscape, the irony of its Raj-inspired address, Goa Way. He cast his eye across neighbouring lawns once planned for garden gnomes, rose beds, and tea-parties, saw instead how they sprouted cylinder heads, hubcaps, big-ends and rear axles and his thoughts drifted to next-door Mrs. Gubbins. Heard her voice crooning though the wall and into his bedroom late on Friday nights, as she extracted promises of shopping trips to Norwich from her drunken husband. Thought of how they were habitually broken next morning by aphasic Mr. Gubbins supine beneath his cherished Mini-Cooper, staring prophetically into a leaking sump, mindless of his daughter Doreen upstairs in her bedroom entertaining the neighbourhood, all pectorals and eye-liner, talking of missed periods and refining techniques of other, more creative, supine postures. Reminded himself of how his neighbours clubbed together like a mafia, shared babies as readily as socket-spanners and had an intimacy with one another some thought responsible for their children's retarded progress through the local primary. Wondered how long it be before the chip fat, Radio 1 and fenland abuse once again woke up to leak beneath the doorways of Goa Way. Felt glad he didn't have a wife to share among them and twelve-year old daughters to counsel in the art of contraception. Then was jolted from his reverie by the surrounding Turkish bath and was reminded that the kettle's automatic shut off didn't work. Was just searching among the previous night's chicken chow-mein for a spoon when there was a knock at the door.

"Come in, matey," Crack hollowed, uncaring who it might be about to breach his property, hands mining the deep strata of dirty plates for a spoon. The door pushed open. A grey-suited office-type, haircut like pencils in a tidy and brandishing a clipboard, efficiently installed himself with short brisk steps among the wilderness of Crack's kitchen.

The history of Wisbech according to Alf Crack

"Mr. Crack," began the man holding up his card as if he were imitating a toothpaste advert, "Bailiff. Come to collect thirty pounds in lieu of Council Tax arrears," now stalking about the kitchen like a heron fishing for minnows, speaking in a grammar school accent with 'O's rounded like Polos and conceit oozing from his cuff-linked sleeves.

"'Ave a perch, ma'ey. Jus' makin' a cuppa." Crack, back to his intruder, searched the sink for the filthiest mug he could find while the bailiff read aloud from his clipboard the tally of missed payments and owed sums, commensurate with their respective dates and accordant penalties.

Ignoring every word of it, Crack fished a mould-encrusted mug from his collection and carried it to the sideboard in such a way the fungus couldn't fail to go unnoticed. Enquiring of his visitor how he took his tea, Crack filled the cup with tea-bag and boiled water, then limped off to the cubby-hole, explaining he was about to breach his life-time savings. Left the bailiff to disappointedly eye his possessionless estate and to wonder why in June, Crack still kept a needleless Christmas tree illuminated with fairy lights. "Man needs head examining," bailiff thought to himself, and spied a crib set out on the window-sill, shepherds and wisemen standing in rank like the painted tin soldiers of a child's Waterloo.

Crack came back five minutes later bearing his coffer. Set down a tea-time assortment biscuit-tin on the table and returned his attention to the fermenting beverage. He dropped a passing comment he was looking forward to Christmas, then having given up on the spoon, searched among his cutlery for a screwdriver to harpoon the tea-bags before stacking them on the accumulating Typhoo pyramid at the end of the sideboard. He fetched last week's milk-carton down off the shelf and put it to his nose, sniffed to check the lactose was just turning tasty, then added the cream cheese and spoonfuls of sugar enough to sink a battleship. Handed the cup of white jelly-fish infested brackish to his guest and suggested they get down to business.

Alf Crack prized the lid from his coffer and a tumble of old postcards fell to the floor. As the bailiff contemplated the Exmouth donkeys and Blackpool nudes, Crack expounded his philosophy of book-keeping and continued to rummage among the litter of his biscuit tin, every now and then illustrating his monologue with irrelevant documents. Sought the bailiff's sympathy with a photo of his gran, "poor ol' gal, died of apple-plexy," and jabbered on about his grandad having been half Lithuanian, wondered if it exempted him from Pole Tax.

The bailiff meanwhile was struggling to hold the mug of fetid tea at arms length, and wondering whether the wetness in the seat of his trousers might be due to Crack's mog having earlier peed on the chair. Certain the kitchen was stinking of cat urine, he hoped he wouldn't have to wait long before the thirty pounds was safely in his hands and he could escape the eccentricities of Crack's habitation.

"'Ere, take a butcher's at this," Crack resumed. "Photo of me ol' man. Played more pranks than 'e ever earned dough."

The bailiff had to resign himself to more of Crack's ramblings.

"Best one he ever did was on Mobbs the chimbly-sweep. I must of been about seven at the time. End of

September it was, and me ol' man was working out Wood Walton way, replacing broken pan-tiles on the Post Office roof. I'd gone along to keep 'im company, excuse for a day off school kind of thing. Then all of a sudden, Mobbs pulls up in his Morris Minor van, painted racing green, "J.R. Mobbs Chimney Sweep" tattooed on its flank, he's come to sweep the chimbly of The Royal Oak. Always did like a tipple did old Mobbs and when he sees me dad half-way up a ladder at the Post Office he hollers out, "How's about a pint of Watney's, Derek?" Had known me dad since they was nippers at the primary. So that way I get to sit in the snooker room, half of ginger beer and bag of pork-scratchings staring at the photos of the Royal Oak darts team. It was getting on for half past two when the landlord asked Mobbs if he'd come to sweep the chimbly or to drink the barrel dry. Dad said we'd best get going ourselves, there was still the ridge-tiles to put right and Reid the Post Office would be wondering where we'd got to.

"Tanked up on Watney's, outside the Royal Oak, me dad has an idea. He fetches his ladder from the front of the Post Office and creeps round the back of the pub. Sends his ladder up the roof, then climbs himself up to the chimbly-stack. Waits for the brush to come up. Meanwhile, Mobbs is down below screwing his rods together, one after the other, sending his brush up the flue. Me dad's waiting at the top, sees the brush coming through and unscrews it off the end of the rods. Hears Mobbs hollering below, must of caught a snack in the chimney but got it clear now. Thinkin' he's got the job done, Mobbs pulls down his rods, unscrewing them one by one. Gets to the end and finds the brush missing. Thinks to his simple self, must of got stuck. Me dad hears the locals, still drinking below, debate the course of action. Consensus is the Royal Oak's chimbly's got a crook in it. Brush must of got stuck in the bend. Mobbs decides to send up Big Bertha, his corkscrew prodder, thinks it will dislodge the brush. Perhaps have to push it out the top. Dad's still up by the stack, sees the corkscrew coming through. Unscrews it from the rods and screws on the brush. Mobbs pulls down his rods, hopes it's done the trick. Gets to the bottom, finds he's lost his corkscrew, but got back his brush. Can't fathom out what the 'ell's going on. Knew he shouldn't of had the fifth jar."

A knock at the door bought Crack to a halt.

"Come in ma'ey," Crack hollowed. Belligerently rather, thought the grey suit.

The door swung open and two burly side-burned men dressed in blue overalls appeared on the threshold.

"Mr. Crack?"

"Hello ma'ey. Come on in. We're jus' 'avin' a cuppa tea. I'm tellin' this 'ere wha's-'is-name about me ol' man."

"Boiled the kettle just in time then," the Eastern Electric man said smugly, and when he saw the quip hadn't registered, he went on bluntly, "We've come to cut you off. Where's your box?" Words sparse in consonants, garnished in thick St. Neots vowels.

"Well I never!" Crack protested as if it were all a flagrant miscarriage of justice which could not possibly befall him.

The bailiff huffed impatiently, saw his thirty pounds delayed by at least half an hour while the Electric men performed their surgery and thought he discerned a certain bravado as Crack entertained the Board. Took the opportunity to remove himself from the chair he was now certain to have been baptised in urine by Crack's cat and poured the contents of his mug over the wildlife growing among the pile of washing-up.

Crack leaned nonchalantly against the kitchen table as the Eastern Electric man lectured him: "Here's what you owe. A hundred and seventeen in unpaid bills. Fifty in call out charges. Ten for disconnection. Seventeen for reconnection. And another fifty for call out when we come to put you back on. Two hundred and forty four in total. We cut you off now, then when you pay up we come back to reconnect you."

Crack's eyes sparkled like two Jiff lemons. He saw his chance like an unguarded wicket.

"Well I was just off to town this morning to get it all paid up. Tell you what. What if I paid up while you chaps hung on here? Then you wouldn't have to come back again. Spare me the second call out charge. Make it only a hundred and ninety seven I owe."

"If you pay up right now, within the next couple of hours."

Crack was already fishing in the biscuit tin for the money whose existence the bailiff had long given up on. Took a bundle of notes from a buff-coloured envelope and counted aloud. Two hundred quid in fresh tenners. Just enough to pay the electric. The bailiff's jaw dropped six inches, saw a morning of waiting in cat-urine stinking kitchen in company of Eastern Electricity. Hollered out a protest.

"Never you mind," Crack assured him, "You can wait in the driveway. I'll call in at work on the way back, collect the arrears. You'll get your money all right. Just a bit of patience."

Crack led his entourage of embezzlers down the garden path, assuring them he'd be back before long, told them to wait right there. He climbed aboard his unlicensed, uninsured, MOT-less Transit van, pointed himself in the direction of March and roared off at full beer. Heard the rattling chassis below and reflected how his faithful Rocinante defied most of the laws of physics as well as those of Her Majesty. Thought to himself he had to raise the money somehow and while he pondered the implausibility and misfortune of it all he might as well have breakfast. He pulled up half a mile later outside Mrs. Grundy's café dreaming of all day breakfast and lashings of sweet tea.

It was ten o'clock by the time he arrived at Newton Cottage, home of the Cambridge professor of Astronomy for whom he had been 'doing the roof' for the last seven weeks, (though he had still to trace the leak which the scientist claimed had been causing him to sleep with a bucket between him and his wife and to dream of Chinese torture).

Just as Crack had hoped, the professor was at home that day, though he was grievously unprepared for the lengthy castigation of the intellectual's greeting. Where on earth had he been for the last week and a half? And since Crack's phone had been cut off, how was a member of the public like himself supposed to get in touch?

Crack, who had turned up only to beg an advance, was leaning against his truck, hands resting on his belly, already having second thoughts about broaching the subject of money. He was only glad to be parked on the pavement and

not in the driveway where two weeks before, the astronomer had eclipsed his escape by parking his Volvo right
across the exit, 'until Crack had done an honest day's
work'. As the scholar rabbitted on about duty, public service, value for money, professional conduct and other such
terms which had long since lost their meaning for Crack,
the builder was already scampering over the duck-boards of
his resourcefulness, searching for a way out of it all. Wondering, firstly, how to get away without physical exertion
and too much lost time, and secondly, how to leave with
money in his pocket.

At pains to placate the irate academic, he set about
acting he was doing something useful. Crawling hippo-wise
over the roof tiles.

Half an hour later, when he heard the star-gazing professor once again humming the tune of Mozart's Jupiter
symphony, and judging him to be suitably mollified, he
came down from his ladder whale-wise to broach the subject of the leak. Explained he'd discovered the likely cause,
a Victorian alteration to the chimney, most likely to con-
venience a rook's nest, meant a blocked up flue, smoke re-
routed through the roof space and out of hole contrived by
missing pan-tile. Would take at least a week to put right.
Meant he had to put a plunger down the chimney to knock
out the offending lime mortar. Cause a lot of mess in the
stove below, might even break the fire bricks. Better not to
risk it and to remove the stove altogether while he under-
took the work. Then, with the stove out of his way he could
put him in a decent RSJ, strengthen up the cottage real
good.

The history of Wisbech according to Alf Crack

The gullible academic looked his workman up and down, had misplaced confidence in the authority of Alf Crack, Est. since 1967, Graduate of City and Guilds, alumnus of six months in Highpoint for tax evasion. But what did he himself know of lime-mortar and chimney breasts, wood-burning stoves and blocked up flues? Thought 'Aresjée', as Crack had called it, must be French for Victorian fireplace. He knew more of other galaxies than life on planet earth and assumed even builders must work by Newton's laws. Expected the universe to unfold the way Einstein said it would, couldn't make allowances for erratic personalities. Eyed Crack as if through a telescope, said that stove had cost him an arm and leg. Didn't want any harm to come to it.

"Exactly," replied Crack. "That's why we should get it out the way before the heavy work starts."

"I suppose if a job's worth doing, it's worth doing properly and if that means removing the stove, so be it," the star-gazer conceded, somewhat placated.

"Got a mate out Chatteris way," Crack dropped in passing, "cleans those wood-burning stoves up real nice. He's doing one for me at the moment. Wouldn't charge a penny for doing yours as well. Seeing as I got to take it out, might as well drop it round at his place. Be done in a week. You won't be needing it any case in this weather."

The castigating scholar of earlier in the morning had cooled like a burnt out star and before he'd finished speaking, he was saying how grateful he was to his all-knowing builder. Found himself helping Alf Crack carry his priceless Victorian relic to the back of Crack's van, believing that with stove out of the way his builder would be able to get down to some hard building labour in the afternoon. Pictured the night when he wouldn't have to sleep with a bucket separating him and his wife. And was immediately disappointed.

"Only one thing," resumed Crack confidently, "my mate only works mornings, better if I get the stove delivered now, come back to start the work this afternoon." And he leapt behind the wheel of his Transit and pointed it in the direction of Ely. Already thinking over the price he'd ask the antiquarian.

Later that morning, Crack sat in the Greasy Spoon, morning work done, seven hundred and fifty pounds better off, having just sold the professor's Victorian relic to the antiquarian in Ely. Hoping the identical one he had seen in the skip out Thrapston way the week before would still be there.

By that time too, he'd been gone from the house three hours and the bailiff and Eastern Electric had just come to blows. Each had been blaming the other for being held up. The bailiff had stated his opinion that if the Board hadn't turned up when they did, he'd have got his thirty pounds within the hour and he'd have been putting his feet up that afternoon. Eastern Electric, of a diverse opinion, believed that Alf Crack was only taking so long on account of having to recover the thirty pounds he had to pay the bailiff. If it weren't for that, they contested, Crack would have been reconnected long ago and they'd all be enjoying a decent cup of tea. The bailiff accused the taller of the two Electric men of interfering with his work and the Electric man retaliated by head-butting him on the nose.

The history of Wisbech according to Alf Crack

The bailiff had to call on neighbour Gubbins for a towel to mop the blood.

It was just after lunch by the time Alf Crack strolled into the Eastern Electric showroom at Market Square, Chatteris, gut bulging from the sausages, pork pie and chips, apple strudel afters, and the two pints of Guinness he'd stopped off at the Falcon to wash it all down with. Leaned over the counter, breathed Stout fumes over the glass and smiled his enormous bucket-handle grin at the obliging assistant, said he had a complaint to make, asked to see the manager. Explained to the obsequious gnome the events of that morning. Said he had just been preparing to leave the house to come and pay up his electric bill when his property was unexpectedly breached by two expletive-wielding thugs dressed in blue overalls, behaving as if they were on the loose from a loony-bin. He was treated to the most foul-mouthed exposition of language he had ever had the misfortune to hear and thought they were about to bludgeon him to death. He was just on the point of phoning the police when they enlightened him they were representatives of Eastern Electric. Almost caused him a heart-attack to hear they were employees of a public service. Said he'd had to stop off at the doctor's on the way for a cardiograph he was so concerned from the shock, and if it hadn't been for the delay in the waiting room he'd have been there at nine-thirty in the morning. Suggested the two offending workers be suspended from duty immediately.

The supervisor came over all apologetic, said he'd personally see to it that the two men were severely reprimanded, had a week's pay docked from their wages, but hoped that his customer hadn't taken too much offence. Then asked if there was anything else he could do for the customer. Alf Crack explained he had a bill to pay up, handed the form under the counter together with the necessary monies. The supervisor counted the grotty notes between his fine soapstone fingers, stamped and signed the form which he slipped back beneath the glass, then fetched two discount vouchers to allay Crack's misfortune, and explained they could be used should the gentleman be considering buying any electrical appliance from their showroom within the next six months. Hoped that Crack wouldn't look badly on the Electric Board's service in future and was sorry for what he'd encountered that morning.

Alf Crack, belly filled with fat conceit, pushed himself through the glass doors of the showroom into the warm summer afternoon and thought he ought to get back home to straighten out affairs.

When Crack roared into Goa Way, just after two thirty in the afternoon, the Electric Board had about given up on him and were on the point of returning to base, while the bailiff was sitting in Gubbins's kitchen still nursing his bleeding nose and blackening eye, explaining to unsympathetic ears how apt he thought the name of the cul-de-sac. He called over the non-existent fence to Alf Crack that he could deal with the Electric Board first.

The two blue overalls grumbled on about how they hadn't had a cup of tea all day and because they hadn't been able to leave the property had eaten no more than a Yorkie bar between them. Wondered why it had taken their customer so long just to drive over to Chatteris. Alf Crack, eyes full of disbelief at such a show of impertinence, explains that after the shock of the morning he'd had to stop off at the doctor's to do a cardiograph, then produces the necessary papers, signed, the Electric men notice, by Managing Director Spark. Hoped to their secret selves that not too many words passed between the two adversaries and set to reconnecting the electric as fast as they could, anxious for a quick escape from Goa Way and a stop-off for a pint at The New Sun Inn.

Ten minutes later they were gone and Crack was once again boiling the kettle. Invited the bailiff to finish off the cuppa he'd started that morning.

Declining the invitation, the bailiff stood on Crack's threshold, saying that if Crack had the money to hand there was no need for him to come in. Alf Crack approached the open doorway where the avian official was stood rook-wise, towel full of ice clutched to his rapidly bulging eye, asking if Crack had a biro he could sign with, since the Electric Board had borrowed his to do the crossword in the Mail and never returned it. Off course, Crack replied, only too willing to oblige.

Taking the scruffy envelope of notes he'd been given by the antiquarian in Ely in exchange for the astronomer's stove, Crack handed it to the bailiff.

"If you just take hold of that ma'ey while I go an' search for a pen."

Left the day's takings to burn a hole in the sweaty palms of his visitor and returned a minute later clutching a pen. He handed the pen to the bailiff to sign his receipt and took back the envelope of money. Removed the wad of crumpled notes from the brown paper package.

The history of Wisbech according to Alf Crack

Alf Crack made sure he eyed the bailiff's face as he fingered through the seven hundred and fifty pounds which not three seconds before, the bailiff himself had his hands on. Knew the bailiff understood the extent of his debts, but by court order was empowered only to take thirty pounds at a time. Noticed how the bailiff's jaw dropped in disbelief. To think that Alf Crack, Est. since 1967, graduate of City and Guilds, habitually insolvent, had got hold of so much money in a day. Watched how the bailiff's fingers shook as he took hold of the pen and wrote out the receipt, while Crack thumbed off three of the greasiest tenners to hand over. Took hold of the receipt and the pen and said he hoped the chap's eye would get better soon, sympathised with him for being on the receiving end of the Electric Board and said good-bye to the man.

Later, left alone in peace, Alf Crack, builder, climbs aboard his Transit van and heads off for Thrapston. He's thinking of the slap up meal he'll treat himself to later in the Fish Bar in Brampton. Two slices of fried cod and a double portion of vinegary chips. Imagines he might stop off on the way back through Huntingdon at Istanbul Kebab, just to get a döner for the road. Then in his mind's eye he sinks five pints of Guinness before closing time at The Black Bull in Wisbech.

Just hoping, hoping, the wood-burning stove identical to the one he took from the scientist, the one he saw in the skip over Thrapston way, would still be there... Imagines it must be. His luck's in today.